In the heart of Entropy, a council of evil met. At their center rose a great, stone pillar—solid black in color, glistening and slick as if coated with oil. The members of the council included a pair of humans concealed beneath black robes; a great red dragon, coiled many times around itself; a ghastly, pale-faced vampire; and many other hideous servants of Entropy.

"The nightshade failed," hissed the dragon. "Now we must be more direct."

"Yes, of course," gurgled one of the black-garbed men. "We shall gain the Crown of Vanderthan by the most ironic method possible—we'll use the humans against themselves. . . ."

Quest Triad
Douglas Niles

Pawns Prevail
Book I

Suitors Duel
Book II

Immortal Game
Book III

Other FIRST QUEST™
Young Readers Adventures

Rogues to Riches
J. Robert King

The Unicorn Hunt
Elaine Cunningham

Son of Dawn
Dixie McKeone

Summerhill Hounds
J. Robert King

First Quest™
Books

Suitors Duel

Book II of the Quest Triad

Douglas Niles

SUITORS DUEL

Copyright © 1995 TSR, Inc.
All Rights Reserved.

Cover concept by Paul Jacquays. Cover art by Den Beauvais.

First Printing: August 1995
Printed in the United States of America
Library of Congress Catalog Card Number: 94-68148

9 8 7 6 5 4 3 2 1

ISBN: 1-56076-922-X

TSR, Inc.
201 Sheridan Springs Rd.
Lake Geneva, WI 53147
United States of America

TSR Ltd.
120 Church End, Cherry Hinton
Cambridge CB1 3LB
United Kingdom

For the sons of Daryhome,
and especially Ian, Paul,
Mark, and David.

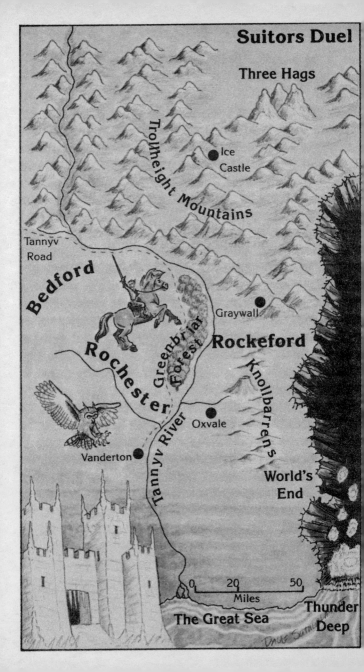

Prologue

Green-swathed hills rolled to the far horizon, crowned by rainbows and fluffy cotton balls of cloud. Waterfalls spilled from the higher crests, vanishing into grottos of white marble or gleaming blue-gray granite. Trout splashed through these waterways, scales rippling like shiny silver coins, while eagles, hawks, and bright doves fluttered through the sun-speckled skies.

Hillside meadows sparkled with thousands of flowers—blossoms of daisy, rose, trillium, columbine, sunflower, and every other beautiful bloom. Amid these meadows grazed deer and tall, slender antelope, unthreatened by predators. After all, this was the realm of those who lived forever, the very grounds of the Immortal Hall itself!

It was a scene of serene perfection—a perfection so total, so complete, that it was almost boring. In fact, thought Dalliphree, it *was* boring.

The fairy buzzed her wings, raising herself from the ground and flitting across the wide plaza surrounding the hall. Everywhere she looked, she beheld a scene of absolute tranquility, complete harmony—and total predictability.

"Why can't something *interesting* happen?" she wondered, veering the course of her hummingbird-like flight through the arched marble entryway, into the halls themselves.

Without really planning her course, she found herself winging toward the great, enclosed garden—probably because that was the place where she had last done anything really interesting. With the memory, she giggled, recalling Pusanth's indignation when the old sage had lost the mortal game to Dalli.

"He's probably *still* sulking!" she whispered to herself with a smirk as she buzzed past the lilac bushes toward the placid goldfish pond. That pool had been the scene of the game, and just coming back here brought back many pleasant thoughts.

"Who's still sulking?" demanded a frail-looking old man, climbing awkwardly to his feet from a bench beside the placid, lily-covered water. When he stood, the fellow's beard trailed almost to his knees—and now it quivered with indignation as he fixed the fairy with a baleful eye.

"Pusanth! You startled me!" objected Dalliphree, ignoring the question.

"Hmph! That's a nice turnabout, for a change," muttered the elder. "Beats having a little girl flying into a person's belly when he's just minding his own business!"

"Oh, you're not still upset about the mortal game, are you?" she asked, batting her long eyelashes.

"I still say I should have won—I *did* win, except my mortal threw the game away at the last minute!"

"But doesn't that mean that *I* won?" Dalli asked innocently.

"All right—*yes!* You won! But you wouldn't win if we did it again!"

The fairy shrugged gracefully, bobbing up and down casually as if it were a matter of no consequence. "You know it wouldn't be fair to the poor mortals—it's bad enough that we meddled with their lives the first time."

"You didn't seem concerned about meddling when you made that artifact," the sage observed sourly.

"The Crown of Vanderthan is an important symbol," Dalli insisted. "The First Daughter will use it wisely, and well."

Pusanth snorted. "Wisdom was not the strongest trait *I* observed in Danis Vanderthan!"

"That's not fair!" For the first time in the teasing conversation, Dalli flushed with emotion. "She chose to place the crown in a safe place and not wear it—*that's* a wise decision!"

"Perhaps it is," Pusanth agreed. "Though if what you say is true, then we have to question your *own* wisdom! You're the one who gave a powerful item to the mortals of Karawenn—a *human,* no less!"

Dalli pouted. The conversation was not going the way she had intended. "Well, we *still* can't play again. I won't do it!"

"Nor did I suggest that you should," Pusanth agreed. "However, I would be so bold as to suggest another wager. It involves our mortals, but in a manner that requires no action from us."

"What wager?" Dalli, still sulking, looked sideways at the old sage.

"Simply this: With *no* interference from us, we allow our two mortals—the First Daughter of Vanderthan and Holton Jaken of Oxvale—to continue their lives on the paths they have chosen."

"What kind of bet is that?"

"I have been watching, thinking. I predict that, before this mortal year is out, their lips will meet in a kiss!"

Dalli gasped, then giggled. "You think that a beautiful princess—one who now owns the most powerful artifact in all Karawenn—would kiss a *farmboy?* Or even *let* him kiss her?"

"Who knows? Maybe *he'll* let her kiss *him!* But

4

yes, the two of them will share that uniquely human gesture of affection, under their own free will."

"Hah! I never thought you were a fool, Pusanth. Stuffy, stodgy, kind of boring sometimes—*definitely* stubborn—but not a fool!"

"Do I detect a note of hesitation?" wondered the sage tauntingly.

"No! I'll take that bet! I just hope you're prepared to lose . . . again."

"I'll take my chances," Pusanth agreed with a dry chuckle.

The pair settled themselves on a stone bench, turning their attention to the goldfish pond. As they stared, the waters grew cloudy. . . .

* * * * *

In the heart of Entropy, a council of evil met. At their center rose a great, stone pillar—solid black in color, glistening and slick as if coated with oil. The members of the council were a varied group, including a pair of humans concealed beneath black robes; a great red dragon, coiled many times around itself; a ghastly, pale-faced vampire; and many other hideous servants of Entropy.

"The nightshade failed," hissed the dragon. "Now we must be more direct."

"How?" demanded one of the wizards, his voice a dry croak.

Suitors Duel

"Simple," replied the massive serpent. "It is time to call upon human agents of Entropy—we have many of them, you know."

"Yes, yes—of course," gurgled the other man, a sound like water bubbling through a partially plugged drain. "We shall gain the Crown of Vanderthan by the most ironic method possible—we'll use the humans against themselves!"

And so it was agreed. The signals, borne by powerful sorcery, traveled from the vile pits of Entropy, through the spheres, making the long journey to the place of men.

There, in Karawenn, those who served the Dark Force heard the summons . . . and they obeyed.

1
A Late Summer Trek

"That'll make a good, smooth rim," Fenrald Fal-whak announced, giving the iron hoop a few ring-ing touches of his hammer. The dwarf turned away from the anvil and stepped to the door of the shed, holding the metal circle in the sunlight. His bearded face creased into a self-satisfied smile as Fenrald admired his handiwork. "Couldn't 'ave done better—well, *much* better, anyway—if I'd used the very forges of Graywall."

"We try to keep our simple shop stocked with the necessities," Derek Jaken said with a chuckle.

Wheeling his chair over to the forge, the legless man reached over to slam shut the vents. "Might as well save the coals—in case we need to heat it up again," he noted.

"That'll depend on your son," the dwarf said with a chuckle. "Is he as fast a worker as he is an eater?"

The weathered face of the chair-bound farmer wrinkled into a good-natured smile. Derek turned toward the shed door as Holton Jaken came in. "How's the wheel coming?" Derek asked.

"Ready for the rim," the young Daryman said, holding up the proof of his own labors. The cartwheel was nearly five feet in diameter, with spokes of smooth oak and a hub of fire-hardened hickory. A curving wooden circle framed the ends of the spokes, but only when the steel rim had been hammered into place would the wheel be complete.

"Let's get this thing put together, then," urged Derek.

Holt passed the wheel to the stocky dwarf, who heated the metal rim slightly and then quickly hammered it into place. The younger Daryman carried the completed wheel out to the trough, where he rolled it through the water, drawing a hiss of steam when the rim first touched the cool liquid. He removed it after the iron hoop seated itself firmly against the wood. Rolling the completed object over to the barn, Holt leaned it beside its twin, which had been completed just this morning.

Derek rolled over to join him, his chair gliding along the plank walkways that Holton had laid between the buildings of the small farm. Fenrald gathered some tools and came after.

The axle should have been iron, they knew, but since they couldn't afford the proper materials, Holt had chiseled a solid, smooth shaft of rock maple. The new cart sat, upside down, waiting only for its wheels.

"This'll do just fine," Fenrald said approvingly, looking at the makeshift axle. "Should be stronger than many a slender piece of metal."

"And a lot easier to come by," Holt agreed.

"What?" Derek teased. "You didn't want to dive off the Market Bridge into the Tannyv River, lookin' for the old one?"

Holt flushed, embarrassed. "I *still* have nightmares about the cart getting stuck—and the princess's men throwing it into the water. I'm almost thinking we should take the new cart all the way to the ferry crossing—instead of using the bridge!"

"Now, lad," Fenrald said. "I think the princess would show a little more patience if you blocked her way again. After all, she *likes* you, now!"

"I'm not taking the chance of blocking *anybody's* way," Holt replied, shuddering. At the same time, very privately, he felt a sense of profound gratitude for that chance encounter on the bridge, unhappy as it had seemed at the time. Then it had been a disaster, as his father's cart and Oxvale's winter batch of cheese had been lost to the flow of the mighty Tannyv. The events had happened only the past spring, but now they seemed like the occurrences of another life.

Since then, however, that chance encounter had taken on a whole new importance. He had come to realize that, if his cart had not gotten stuck and blocked the path of the royal party, Holt would never have met Princess Danis, First Daughter of Vanderthan.

As the pleasant days of this summer had passed, he found himself thinking about her more and more, remembering each detail of her golden hair, her eyes of aquamarine. They had come to trust each other, each in their own stubborn fashion, and together with loyal companions like Fenrald they had saved Karawenn from a dire threat. At the same time, Holt realized, they had become friends.

"Hello, neighbors! What's for dinner?" A stooped, rotund man limped into the yard, collapsing to sit on the cart harness as if the walk up the lane had fully exhausted him. The fellow mopped his sweating brow with a rag, grimacing.

"Hello, Nowell," Holt said with a sigh. "I think there's still some of that goose left—and whatever my fishnets have snared from the stream." The neighboring farmer, who was known as 'Nowell the Aching' behind his back, brightened perceptibly.

Douglas Niles

"The trout are running early this year. We should have a proper feast—in honor of your trip to the city, of course."

"Of course," Derek said cheerfully. "And you're welcome to join us—of course!"

"As if we could get rid of him!" Holt muttered under his breath to Fenrald. He really didn't mind helping out with Nowell's chores, but tonight he would have enjoyed a meal with just his father and the dwarf.

A huge draft horse, free to graze in the yard, clopped over to the cart.

"Old Thunder looks dubious," Derek observed. "He's enjoyed a summer outside of the cart-harness."

"You won't mind a trip to the city, will you?" Holt asked, giving the horse an affectionate clap on the shoulder. The big gelding nickered appreciatively.

Within a few minutes the wheel hubs had been secured to the axle. Holt applied liberal scoops of grease, and then he and Fenrald righted the sturdy wagon, heaving it onto its wheels.

"And you can check the nets with still an hour to spare till supper," Derek declared, delighted.

And a day to pass before I see the princess again. The thought came to Holt with such vivid force that he sighed audibly, catching his foot on the harness and tripping, facedown, to the ground. He was still smiling absently as he got up and dusted himself off.

Suitors Duel

* * * * *

In the end there was no question of taking the ferry—Holt was too impatient to take the long detour. Old Thunder trundled the cart steadily down the road, pulling Derek and an assortment of cheeses while Holt and Fenrald ambled along on foot. In a scabbard at the young man's side rested the Lodestone Blade, sword of his ancestors. The dwarf bore his battered hammer in similar readiness, though there should be no real threat on the road between Oxvale and Vanderton.

They reached the bridge and crossed without incident, and the young Daryman's heart pounded as they found themselves on the lanes below the alabaster heights of Castle Vanderthan. From the high tower fluttered all three banners, signifying that the king, the queen, and the First Daughter were all within that imposing palace.

"We'll get ourselves settled at the Red Salmon," Derek said. "I'll keep the cheese and the cart under watch if the two of you want to visit the castle."

"You're coming with us, Father," Holt said. "We'll hire somebody to watch the cart."

Derek blinked, then shook his head. "I don't have any wish to see that castle," he declared. "You young fellas go."

Fenrald joined Holt in persuading, and finally Derek's surprisingly strong protestations were overridden.

Douglas Niles

The Red Salmon was an inn they had stayed at before on their infrequent visits to the city, and now they made their way along the waterfront streets until they saw the familiar, weathered sign—a wooden board sawed into a fish shape, treated with red paint a very long time ago.

The innkeeper, Old Agad, was a cheery, plump fellow. He immediately ushered the three travelers to a comfortable room—one of a few on the ground floor, to accommodate the farmer's chair. "It has been too many years, my good Daryman," he said. "Can you join me for a quiet mug beside my fireplace?"

"Later," Derek assured him. "Now, it seems we have business at the palace. Can't keep royalty waiting, can we?" he added, with a wink at Holt. "But I'll ask you," the farmer added. "What should we do with the cart while we're gone, and overnight?"

"Little Agad will keep an eye on it for you," Agad declared. "We'll park it right outside the stables."

"Very good!" agreed Derek, rolling toward the door with a flourish.

Holt was not too certain about the guarding abilities of someone called "Little Agad" until he met the innkeeper's son. The young man hulked a good half a foot over the Daryman—who was himself unusually tall, if a little scrawny. Little Agad, by contrast, was a strapping fellow with shoulders like a bull and arms that rippled and bulged with sinew. In return for a piece of silver, he promised to feed and water Old Thunder, and to guard the Darymen's possessions while they were gone.

"Let's cut across the market," Holt said eagerly. He would normally have wanted to tour the multitude of shops and stalls there; now he saw the market as the shortest route to the palace.

Pushing his father's chair, he led Fenrald into the wide plaza that filled a long, curving plateau between the river and the heights where the castle dominated. They circled around a huge expanse, where shepherds and weavers from Bedford were displaying a selection of brightly colored cloaks. They pushed between fruit and meat vendors from the surrounding hills and brewers offering kegs of yeasty ale. An unmistakable smell signaled the little shop where a fisherman offered silvery salmon and speckled trout.

Though the market was not terribly crowded, there were enough people that Holt occasionally had to wait for the crowd to thin before he could advance with the rolling chair. They had nearly crossed the plaza when a great crowd of women blocked the path, clamoring around a baker's booth where a multitude of fresh pies had just arrived.

Looking for a way around, Holt saw a flash of silver, and was intrigued by the sight of a withered old woman, stooped and frail, whose arms and neck were encircled by a variety of glimmering chains. She stood beside a small cart that was bedecked with a variety of silver goods—bracelets, necklaces, rings, and chains.

"Here's for you," she offered with a persuasive wink at a tall warrior who stood before her. The man, with his back to Holt, nodded and leaned forward, pulling the chain over his wrist.

Holt suddenly thought he should take Danis some kind of gift, a token of his joy at their reunion. Of course, he had few coins in his purse; but perhaps there was something. He stepped closer to the silver-laden cart, waiting for the warrior to finish.

"Remember, be prepared to remove the bar when you receive the white pigeon," the fellow was saying to the hag, using the first three fingers of his left hand to point toward the distant sky. "Not before!"

Amused by the unusual snatch of conversation, Holt was wondering about prices when another flash of silver caught his eye—from the other side of the woman's cart.

He watched, instinctively suspicious, as a hooded figure moved along the wares of silver. He saw a slender hand reach out, hefting a number of chains as if evaluating their weight and quality. Then the cloaked stranger laid one of the chains back down and turned away.

Holt hadn't seen the other chains disappear, but he was certain that the fellow had picked up more of the silver goods than he had set down.

"Hey!" cried the Daryman, amazed at the theft.

The hooded figure whirled, and Holt got an impression of two huge, brown eyes—wide with shock and staring directly at him. Then the figure darted away, cutting around women bickering over pies.

"Stop! Thief!" Holton lunged after the culprit.

He was struck by the unnatural grace of the hooded figure—almost as if he flowed across the ground instead of ran in a series of steps. Still, the fellow was smaller than Holt, and the Daryman was a fast sprinter. Though he wore his sword, Holt did not draw the weapon, keeping his hands free for balance.

With fluid grace, the thief skidded around a corner, and perhaps he would have escaped—except that a shepherd of Bedford chose that moment to drive his flock into the aisle. The fleeing cutpurse stumbled into the tightly packed animals, and in another instant Holt hit him from behind with a flying tackle.

Both of them tumbled to the cobblestones, in the midst of panicked, bleating sheep. The Daryman felt the thief's arms under his loose cloak and quickly pulled the fellow's hands behind his back. In another instant Fenrald was there—apparently the dwarf's grim visage convinced the culprit that any attempt at escape was useless.

"I saw you steal those—silver things," Holt charged. "Now, come with me—you can give them back to the lady before I take you to the magistrate!"

"Actually, I only took one bracelet—*this* one," the thief replied in surprisingly cultured tones. He held out a thick ring of silver, which Holt snatched away, noting that the bracelet was surprisingly scratched and worn.

"Well, you are coming with us, at any rate," said Fenrald firmly. He and the farmer prodded the culprit back toward the cart.

They met Derek wheeling after them, his face tight with concern—until he saw that Fenrald and his son had matters well in hand.

"Looks like you picked the wrong time for your thievery," the older Daryman said, wagging a finger at the cutpurse, who nodded, pleasantly enough, in agreement.

"Let's see what that old woman has to—" Holt stopped as they came around the bakery shop. The crowd had thinned a bit, but he clearly remembered the spot where the hag had sold her wares. There was no sign of her, nor her cart, nor the warrior who had been her customer.

It was as if they had never been there at all.

2
Syssal Kípícan

"I wouldn't be surprised if they're out of the city by now," the thief remarked as Fenrald and Derek sought vainly for a sign of the silver-merchant or her cart. The fellow's voice was smooth and articulate—and apparently more resigned than resentful regarding his capture.

"What do you mean?" demanded Holt suspiciously. "I saw you take that bracelet from her—why should *she* be the one to flee?"

The thief shrugged. "Just a guess," he explained.

"No sign of 'em—like they sank right through the ground," Fenrald groused, clumping back to his companion. Derek, too, wheeled back with a negative report.

"Who are you, anyway?" the young Daryman asked, warily eyeing his captive. Holt's right hand remained near the hilt of the Lodestone Blade, while his left kept a firm grip on the rascal's collar. Still, he felt just a little ridiculous—something told him that the thief was not about to make an attempt at escape.

"Syssal Kipican, at your service." Removing his hood to reveal a wealth of curling, golden hair, the captive blinked those huge eyes again, and then swept forward into a graceful bow. "And my congratulations on your alertness and decisive reactions," he added. "Though the cost, it would seem, is to me."

"An elf!" spat Fenrald Falwhak, squinting up at the slender thief's face. "You're an elf, or I'll shave my beard!"

"No need for a razor, old fellow," Syssal replied pleasantly. He drew his flowing hair back to the nape of his neck, revealing the slender ears, tapering to narrow points, that were the characteristic features of his race.

"I—I've never met an elf before," Holt said in surprise and delight before he recalled the circumstances. "That is, I've never *captured* an elf before."

"And to whom do I owe the honor of my apprehension?"

"I'm Holton Jaken, of Oxvale. This is my father,

Derek; and that's Fen—"

"I'm the war chief of Graywall!" blurted the dwarf, his face flushing as he glowered at Syssal. "And I have no words for elves!"

Holt had never seen his companion so upset. "He stole only a bracelet," the Daryman whispered. "Nobody was killed, or even hurt!"

"He's an *elf!*" hissed the dwarf. "And an elven thief, at that! I think we should—"

"We're taking him to the castle," Holton declared, firmly cutting off whatever gruesome suggestion Fenrald had been about to make. "We'll let the First Daughter—or the king—decide what to do with you."

"The castle?" Syssal's eyebrows raised in a gesture of surprise, and—perhaps—curiosity. "This is growing more interesting by the moment."

"There're a few questions *I'd* like to ask," Derek said quietly as Holt prepared to usher the thief from the market. "Like—why did you think that silver-merchant would be gone when we got back here?"

"People such as her are afraid of the light, afraid of the attention that must result from the commotion I—that is, *we*—caused."

"But why?" Holt wondered

"Quite simple. The bracelet in question is *my* property. I don't know how the hag came into possession of it, but it is a thing of great importance to me. It was not a question of want—I *needed* to get it back."

"Why didn't you offer to buy it back? You don't look like a beggar—surely you have a coin or two that you could have used to make the purchase?" pressed Holt while Fenrald glared skeptically.

"Actually, I'm rather penniless at the moment. Though even if I carried a bulging coin purse, I suspect that she would not have sold it to me."

"Why not?"

"For reasons too complicated to go into right now. Perhaps we will have an occasion where we can discuss the issue in greater depth. Actually, I wouldn't mind that, at all."

"Why, you insolent cutpurse!" snarled Fenrald, his hand tightening around his battered hammer. "You'll talk *now*—or I'll do some persuading!"

"We should get going," Holt said hastily, fearing the hot-tempered dwarf's intentions. "Let's get to the palace—then we can talk!"

"You'll have *plenty* of time for that when they lock you in the dungeon!" grumbled the dwarf, prodding the elf after Holt.

Derek wheeled himself as the dwarf and the young Daryman escorted the prisoner across the plaza to the foot of the steep hill. Though the roadway was fairly smooth, it was obvious to them all that the proud farmer was having difficulty pushing up the incline.

"Allow me to help," Syssal said, with an eyebrow raised toward Holt. "That way you two can keep a firm grip on my arms."

"I don't trust this weasel!" Fenrald blurted before Holt could reply.

"Perhaps I intend to escape using the aid of this racing vehicle?" the elf inquired mockingly.

Fenrald glowered even more savagely, but said nothing further as Syssal took the handles of the chair and started to push. The little party made its way up the winding, climbing streets of Vanderton, rising from the common marketplace and teeming, popular inns past residences of increasing splendor. Soon they turned a corner and saw a grand stone facade lined with white marble columns.

"The royal mint," Syssal noted, as Holt flushed—embarrassed that this thief could give him information about the city. "A work of architectural magnificence—one of humanity's great achievements."

Fenrald was about to scoff, but he squinted at the columns and the wide steps, and was forced to nod in grudging agreement. "It's not dwarven work," he admitted, "but it's good, solid—and functional."

Holt knew that his dwarf friend had praised the building in unusually glowing terms. "The castle's even better," he promised, feeling the need to prove a little of his own familiarity with Vanderton.

In a few minutes his words were proven as they came around a corner and saw the full glory of Castle Vanderthan rising before them. Both the keep and the outer wall were surfaced with white quartz that now, in the late afternoon sun, glowed with a pearly luster. A deep moat yawned before them, while the pennants atop the castle tower, fully sunlit, streamed like flames from their staffs.

Soon they reached the gatehouse, where the drawbridge was lowered across the moat. As they trundled across the planks, Holt saw a company of guards lounging in the shade of the structure's arched passageway. Memories of his first visit came back as he recognized the guardpost sergeant who swaggered into the roadway to confront them. The big, bearded fellow had been an unpleasant bully on that occasion—he didn't look to have changed over the summer.

Instinctively Holt threw his shoulders back and stalked forward to meet the man's squinting, piglike gaze.

"Please convey to Princess Danis, First Daughter of Vanderthan, that Holton Jaken—a Daryman of Oxvale—has come to call upon her."

For a moment the guard stared in disbelief, until he doubled over with a guffaw of laughter. His companions in the gatehouse chorused in amusement.

"Why do you want to see her?" the men hooted. "To milk her cows? With a dwarf for your stable-boy, and a flower-maker and a cripple to help?"

Holt flushed. Instinctively his hand went for the hilt of his sword, but he held back when he felt

Derek's calm touch upon his wrist. He fought for the control to speak when Fenrald stepped forward, speaking conversationally to the still-chortling guard.

"I've seen cows, and steers, and pigs during my summer in Oxvale—but there was not one of them more stupid, nor even *half* as ugly, as yourself."

The human's laughter ceased abruptly, his hand going for the heavy sword at his belt. Before he touched the weapon the dwarf seized the guard's beard and jerked his head down until they were face-to-face. The man struggled vainly to break Fenrald's grip as the dwarf spoke.

"This young farmer is the man who found the Crown of Vanderthan, and gave it to Princess Danis—who also happens to be a fond friend of *mine!* She *will* want to see us. Now, if you don't want to spend the rest of yer days guarding sewer rats on the waterfront, you'll see that she knows we're here!"

At last Fenrald released the man's beard. The fellow stumbled backward, eyes bulging as his hands touched his chin as if pushing his strained whiskers back into place. "I—I'll see that she finds out—right away!" he stammered, spinning on his heel and all but running across the courtyard.

In a short while he came back with a familiar figure—one of childlike size, but with the wizened face of an elder and the flowing sideburns to match.

"Gazzrick!" cried Holt, leaving Syssal to Fenrald's care as he stepped forward to clasp the halfling in an embrace.

"The princess will be along shortly," declared Gazzrick Whiptoe, who was a royal adviser to the king—and had been the lifelong tutor of the First Daughter.

"She said I should take you to the garden—we're to make ourselves comfortable. And Fenrald, too, of course—and this must be your father," the halfling added with a gracious bow. "And yourself, sir?" he asked Syssal Kipican.

"I'm a thief, under escort so that the princess, presumably, may pass judgment," the elf explained helpfully. "Pleased to make your acquaintance."

"The, er, same," replied Gazzrick, with a questioning look at Holt. The Daryman described the encounter in the marketplace, though he was finding the elf more and more a puzzle. Certainly Syssal did not seem like a typical criminal, if there was such a thing.

"Well, come along then," the halfling offered, leading the group past the guards—all of whom bowed low.

Fenrald and Holt each retained a grip on Syssal's sleeve, while Derek wheeled beside Gazzrick in the lead. They passed between a pair of high hedges, and then the palace adviser led them around a series of sharp corners, flanked by high greenery, and through several intersections. Despite the complexity of the path, the halfling jogged along quickly—once Holt bumped into Syssal as they went around a corner in their hurry to keep Gazzrick in sight.

"We're going back to the Queen's Walk," Gazzrick said. "It's out of the way—a good place for a chat."

"I'll agree it's out of the way," Fenrald grumbled. "It's got me about turned into knots."

"Ah, here we are," Gazzrick said, rounding another sharp corner. Holt, looking up at the flowering hedges, gave Syssal's sleeve a pull and stepped after the halfling.

"Quit tugging, elf!" snapped Fenrald, pulling back. Holt and the dwarf whirled in surprise, standing nose to nose and holding each other's shirts.

There was no sign of Syssal Kipican.

"How did he do that?" Fenrald blustered, whirling through a circle while Holt sprinted back to the last intersection. Four corridors twisted away between the hedges; none of them offered any sign of the elf.

"He got away?" inquired Gazzrick hesitantly. "We brought a thief into the Queen's Walk, and he *escaped?*" The halfling's face took on an unhealthy shade of gray.

"Yes, he did," Holt admitted grimly. He tried to console the halfling. "Though I'd guess he's not much of a danger to anyone. He seemed a surprisingly decent fellow, actually." Even as the words left his mouth, the Daryman noticed that his dagger was missing. Had Syssal snatched it from his belt?

"I'd better notify the guards. What was his crime?" asked the halfling, starting toward the path.

"He stole this—" Holt reached for the pouch at his belt, but his heart sank as he touched the supple outlines of the small, and currently empty, sack.

Like the thief and Holt's dagger, the silver bracelet was gone.

3
A Meeting, and More Meetings

"Holt! Holt! You're here! And Fenrald! It's so good to see you, my friends! Welcome—a hundred times welcome!"

The Daryman's heart leapt into his throat as he heard the words, the voice still as familiar as if he'd spoken with the princess only yesterday. She raced into the garden through a gap in the hedge and gave the Daryman a hearty hug before turning to clap Fenrald on the shoulder and introduce herself to Derek.

"Princess! Danis!" Holt stammered, his mind too

giddy to allow him to form phrases. Instead he looked at her, his face locked in a beaming expression of delight. By all the spheres, how could he have forgotten how beautiful she was?

Danis Vanderthan's hair was the yellow of spun gold, and it coiled about her shoulders in a lush cascade. Her aqua eyes were the deep color of a placid mountain pool, and when she smiled at Holt her happiness was like the warm glow of the sun. Yet she quickly turned away, as if a secret sadness would enter her eyes if she saw him a moment longer. Holt was made a little uneasy by the look, but his momentary concern vanished as another familiar voice pulled his attention around.

"Whooo has come to visit?" The Daryman waved at the large, broad-winged owl gliding into the garden behind the princess.

"Sir Ira! How are you?"

"Why, splendid as ever, I should say. And you're looking well—though I see you're still keeping a certain disreputable company," the owl added, blinking sagely at Fenrald Falwhak.

"If it isn't my favorite bag of feathers," the dwarf chuckled. "And as well stuffed with hot air as ever!"

"Ho, my dear—is this the young Daryman, then?" asked a pudgy man who strolled into the garden after the owl. Holt had to look twice to convince himself that this must indeed be the king of Vanderthan. Thinning white hair covered the fellow's pink scalp, and his close-shaved whiskers were equally pale. His long, trailing robe of deep blue and the golden belt encircling his ample belly were the clearest proof of his royal status.

"Father, I present Holton Jaken, Fenrald Falwhak, and Derek Jaken; gentlemen, King Dathwell Vanderthan," said Danis solemnly. "Though I thought I heard from the gatesman that there were four of you," she added, turning back to Holt.

"We were—that is . . ." With a sigh, knowing he would sound like an utter fool, Holt repeated the tale of Syssal Kipican. "He's in here somewhere—he got away from us in the hedges. I-I'm terrible sorry. He wanted that bracelet awfully badly. Oh, and Gazzrick went to tell the guards."

"He'll turn up, then—no worries," declared the king with a dismissive wave. "Derek Jaken!" he declared heartily, stepping up to Holt's father. "It is good to see you again, my man."

"And you as well, Sire," replied the elder Daryman. "And especially pleasing for me that it can be in the company of my son."

Holt stared, shocked to learn that his father *knew* King Dathwell, and on a fairly warm basis to judge by the monarch's tone of voice. Puzzled, he wondered why Derek had been so reluctant to come up to the castle.

"And tell us about yourself, lad," the monarch added, peering closely at the Daryman. Despite the man's befuddled appearance, Holt saw that his eyes—a paler blue than his daughter's—were clear and sharp.

"Holt is the guide who led us through the Knollbarrens on the quest for the Crown," Danis said, smoothly stepping forward to his rescue. "Then, when we reached Graytor Castle, it was Holt who penetrated the depths of the caves there, and found the crown . . . and allowed me to return home with it."

"Indeed—he proved to be a lad of ingenuity and courage," Sir Ira chimed in.

The king nodded, not displeased. "You are a Daryman, I understand—from Oxvale?"

"Yes, Your Majesty," Holt said proudly.

"Your people have a long history of courage and service," King Dathwell Vanderthan remarked. "As well, I suppose, as a noted tendency toward stubborn self-rule. Still, I have long admired the Darymen."

"Thank you, Sire," the young farmer replied, wondering at the king's odd compliment—if, in fact, it had been intended as praise.

"Say," continued the monarch with elaborate nonchalance, "Oxvale is one of the villages praised for its cheese, is it not?"

"Yes, Your Majesty. My village has earned a certain reputation in that area."

"Is it possible that you brought some of that delectable stuff with you? Even, perchance, a bit of the Fisher Sharp?"

"Your Majesty," offered Derek Jaken, wheeling

forward and bowing with a flourish. "There is a large block of Karl Fisher's finest in our cart—and as of this moment, it is intended for none other than yourself!"

"Splendid! Oh, that really *is* nice! Now, do you have accommodations in town?"

Derek replied in the affirmative.

"You must cancel them—I insist that you (and your cheese, of course) come up to the castle as my guests! You will stay here so long as you are in the city!"

"Th—Thank you, Your Majesty!" said Holt, delighted with the offer. He finally relaxed a little, feeling that the meeting with the king was progressing rather well.

A fanfare of trumpets arose from across the garden. "That must be the grand procession!" declared the king, gesturing for the others to follow him. "Come along, all of you. Did Danis tell you that your timing couldn't have been better? Tonight, there shall be a spectacular feast! It is an occasion for great celebration!"

Before Holt could speak, the king had swept out of the garden, the other companions hurrying in his wake.

"What's going on?" the Daryman asked the princess, jogging to catch up with her.

Danis sighed and shrugged her shoulders. "My father's having a contest—and I assume that the contestants have arrived." He sought some further clue in her expression, but she kept her eyes facing the front—almost as if she didn't want to meet his gaze.

His momentary uneasiness returned, but Holt could learn nothing more until they passed through the hedges of the garden and emerged into the wide courtyard before the keep's main doors. A crowd of courtiers and ladies had assembled, and before them stood a rank of heralds with brass trumpets. Five elegantly dressed men held staffs with flowing banners—but these pennants were currently lowered so Holt couldn't see the images emblazoned upon them.

King Dathwell ascended a set of wide, marbled steps leading to the portico and balcony before the palace doors. He turned to urge his daughter up to his side. Instinctively the Daryman held back—not just because his father's chair was blocked by the steps, but because he sensed that he did not belong up there.

The Daryman felt a tug at his sleeve and looked down to see Gazzrick Whiptoe. The halfling scratched at one of his sideburns; like Danis, he seemed vaguely uncomfortable.

"What is it? What's going on around here?" demanded Holt.

"Going on? Well, er . . . in fact, I just spoke with the captain of the guards. His men have thoroughly searched the gardens and the stables. There doesn't seem to be any sign of the thief. He's probably gone over the wall, sneaked back into the city."

"Over the wall? That wall is at least thirty feet high!" the Daryman objected. "How could he get out?"

"Well, it's high on the outside," Gazzrick demurred. "But there's lots of places, when you're *inside* the castle, that you can climb right up to the top—on stairways to the watchposts, or through any of the towers. Once he got to the top, he could have lowered a rope and made an easy getaway."

"He didn't *have* a rope!"

"Well, maybe he found one. In any event, it doesn't seem like he's still in the castle."

"Well, that's a relief, I guess." Holt, in fact, didn't feel relieved. He wished that someone had seen the thief make his getaway—at least he wouldn't worry that he had brought a dangerous character into the castle and then let him escape to work mischief. Well, maybe not dangerous, he told himself, but certainly mysterious.

Abruptly, his thoughts returned to the courtyard. Gazzrick had started to sidle away, and Holt clapped a friendly but firm hand on the halfling's shoulder. "You're not trying to avoid me, are you? Danis would hardly look at me when we came around the castle, and now you're sneaking off! What kind of a welcome is this?" he teased.

The halfling blushed, then stammered an apology. "I—I guess the king doesn't need me up there.

Very well—let's go into the castle and find a comfortable place to talk."

"What about this?" Holt gestured to the courtyard. The people now thronged to the sides, leaving a wide, clear expanse from the gates to the portico. "Why won't anyone tell me what's going on?"

"Er, that is, I think we'll see soon enough."

The king and Danis—and a graceful, white-haired woman whom Holt guessed must be the queen—stood with an assortment of courtiers and nobles before the keep. Across the courtyard, the portals of the mighty gatehouse stood open, the drawbridge still lowered across the moat. Abruptly the heralds blew a long blast on their horns, and Gazzrick gestured toward the castle gates.

One of the squires raised a pennant of blue, and as it snapped outward in the wind the symbol of a broad-winged hawk was revealed.

A man mounted astride an elaborately robed war-horse came through the gate and guided his proud steed on a circuit before the assemblage. The fellow was tall and strikingly handsome, with golden hair swept back from his lean, hardened face. He wore a cloak of blue that matched the blankets over his horse, and his silver breastplate was adorned with the image of a falcon in the same color.

"A welcome to the first contestant!" cried one of the heralds, reminding Holt that Danis had mentioned something about a contest being held by her father. Untying a blue ribbon, the crier unrolled a scroll of parchment and read from the page.

"Prince Gallarath, Son of Rochester, Slayer of the Blue Gorgon, and First Son of the King of Rochester! Prince Gallarath is the Master of the Battle-axe, and he bids a welcome to the king and queen of Vanderthan—and to their lovely daughter. He would like it known that word of Danis Vanderthan's beauty and grace has extended even so far as Rochester!"

Holt felt a flush of fury as he watched the rider's smug, arrogant countenance. Completing his circuit of the courtyard, the prince dismounted and strode confidently up the steps to greet the royal family of Vanderthan. The king and queen were delighted, but the Daryman was somewhat mollified to see Danis's decidedly cool greeting.

Horns blared again, and another rider—this one clad in flowing crimson emblazoned with the symbol of a black stag—swept through the gates at an easy canter. The crier consulted a scroll wrapped in a red ribbon.

"Earl Terrence Degraine, Lord of Amana, Slayer of the Black Stag! Earl Terrence is Master of the Crossbow, and has journeyed from the valleys below the Icepeak Mountains for the opportunity to accept the king of Vanderthan's most gracious invitation!"

Like the prince, Earl Terrence guided his proud charger through a circle so that everyone present could admire him before he, too, drew up before the gates of the keep and dismounted. The earl paused to dust the grit of the trail from his boots, trousers, and gloves, before he turned toward the king and ascended the steps.

Already the trumpets blared again, and with a resigned sigh Holt looked at the gate, preparing for the next of the contestants—though he was certain he didn't really want to see.

Sir Erik Merriwell, Slayer of the Bull Troll, Grand Knight of Rockeford, and Master of the Sword, was clad in black and emblazoned with the outline of a gray wolf. Seeing the knight's mane of silver-gray hair and a beard to match, Holt realized that Sir Erik was older than the other contestants—though he rode with the wiry agility of a much younger man. A high-ranking noble from the Duchy of Rockeford, Sir Erik spared the crowd the promenade—a fact that warmed Holt's reaction, a trifle. Instead the knight rode directly to the Vanderthans and dismounted. His black armor was dusty from the road, and when he clapped his gloves together more dust flew from them. Despite the late summer heat, the knight kept his gloves on as he climbed the steps and took his place beside the prince and the earl.

Next to ride through the gates was Baron Durqueson of Ironwood. Holt scowled through the accolades—Master of the Lance, Slayer of the White Gargoyle, and so forth. The baron wore a white tunic and a cloak that looked, admittedly, quite dashing. He had a broad smile, framed by a neatly trimmed beard, and his long, dark hair had been combed and oiled until it glowed. His symbol, on breastplate and pennant, was a leering face rendered in black outline—the gargoyle, no doubt. Durqueson dragged out his promenade through two full circuits around the courtyard, winking rakishly at a crowd of giggling maidservants before he dismounted and all but swaggered up the steps to the Vanderthans.

Another blast of horns—the sound was beginning to grate on Holt's nerves—brought the next contestant into the courtyard. Lord Bluth Terragal, Ambassador and High Minister of Bedford, was a huge man, with a full beard that swept in a tangle across his chest. He was approaching middle age, to judge from the lines on his well-fed face, and the traces of gray in his hair and beard. Wearing a brown robe, the lord was introduced as the Slayer of One Hundred Goblins. His symbol was the elk—though to Holt it looked very much like the stag of Earl Terrence.

The lord took his huge horse around a large circle, so close to the onlookers that globs of mud flew from the great hooves to spatter the same servant girls who had giggled at Baron Durqueson. Clumping his heavy boots, the lord dismounted, marched up the steps and clapped a startled King Vanderthan on his shoulder.

Suitors Duel

Hesitantly, fearing what he would see next, Holt turned back to the gate—but no trumpet call sounded, and no further contestants seemed to be expected. Indeed, the king and his family soon ushered the five men into the castle.

Glumly, the Daryman looked to his companions. Never before, it seemed, had his humble roots weighed so heavily on him. How would he even have a chance to talk to Danis with all these noblemen crowding around? Plus, he hadn't liked the way that several of them had looked at her. His mood grew darker as he pondered the emotions veiled by those manly glares.

"What kind of contest is the king going to hold?" Derek asked Gazzrick as the crowd dispersed around them.

The halfling shrugged. "The king has kept that a secret—though he has promised to make the announcement at dinner tonight. He's holding a grand feast, you know—and you're all invited to be there, of course."

"If the contest is a secret, why did these fellows ride from so far away to take part in it?" Holt asked sourly.

Gazzrick, again, wouldn't meet his eyes. Holt had a sick feeling in the pit of his stomach, but he gently placed a hand on the halfling's shoulder. "Please—tell me?"

"Well, er . . . it's nothing definite. More like things that have been indicated, guesses made, that sort of thing. . . ."

"What do you mean?" insisted Holt.

"Well, just this. I think—it seems, well, that the king is going to promise that the winner of the contest . . . er, that he will gain the hand of the king's daughter, that is, in marriage."

4
A Royal Repast

Holt found a way to keep himself busy as the afternoon hours slipped into evening. The feast would begin several hours after dark, so the Daryman decided that he'd have time to fetch the cheese that the king had requested. Besides, it gave him a chance to get out of the palace.

He and Fenrald returned to the Red Salmon and, after tipping the elder and younger Agads for their trouble, hitched the cart to Old Thunder and took the cheese up to the castle. The guards at the gatehouse let them pass without question this time—a good thing, Holt reflected, since in his current mood he would have been tempted to cross blades with someone at the slightest provocation.

The dwarf sensed his melancholy and didn't try to cheer him up with trite pronouncements. Instead, Fenrald griped about the weather, about the steep climb, about all manner of trivial and insignificant problems, until finally the Daryman was forced to laugh—if a trifle wanly.

"You'd think they could keep the cobblestones flush with the courtyard!" the dwarf groused as they at last clopped toward the palace stables.

"They look pretty flat to me," the Daryman replied.

"Hah—shows what humans know. I just about tripped over one that stuck up a good quarter inch above the rest. You'd never find that with dwarven workmanship, I assure you."

Old Thunder hauled the cart into the stable, and the pair, working easily together, unhitched the big draft horse and removed his harness and tack. "One thing you humans do pretty well," Fenrald admitted, as he started pulling wheels of cheese out of the cart, "is make food. There, you could teach some of the dwarven masters a thing or two."

"That reminds me," Holt said. "You promised to take me to Graywall someday so I could see your town, meet your kinsmen. You know, I'd really like to do that—sometime soon."

"Like tonight?" Fenrald asked, softly teasing.

"Well, soon, anyway! There's nothing for me here—that's pretty plain, now."

"Don't talk like that, lad. Why, these fops and fools aren't going to keep Princess Danis away from her old friends! We got lots of catching up to do, and I know—"

"I know that even seeing her again is going to kill me!" Holt wailed, shaking his head miserably. "By all the spheres, Fenrald—it's not like I ever expected to *marry* her, or anything like that! But how can I even show my face at the table when she's surrounded by such a crowd of overdressed peacocks? Should I wear my milking shirt? Maybe my woodcutter's trousers will turn all eyes my way!"

"Er, I couldn't help overhearing," Gazzrick said from the door of the stable. "And perhaps I can set at least that concern to rest. Garments have been provided for you—though they are not, quite, of the 'peacock' style. Still, I've done my best to get things that will fit. They are even now in your sleeping chamber, where your father has been making himself quite comfortable, I might add. I came looking for you, to see if I could show you where you'll be staying."

"Thanks, Gazzrick," Holt said. "Yes—the clothes and the guiding would be much appreciated. And whatever you've found for us will be fine. To tell you the truth, I'm not much in the mood for silken finery."

"Yes . . . I can quite imagine. It *is* unfortunate that

your visit fell on this day, of all times. Still, I know that the princess was delighted to see you—she asked about you after the ceremony. She would have left the nobles standing about while she went to find you if her father had let her have her way."

The halfling led them into the keep, and Holt—in spite of his dour mood—was awed by the splendor of the grand entry hall. The ceiling overhead was higher than the biggest house in Oxvale, and the walls of white stone were draped with tapestries depicting hunts, battles, royal ceremonies, and pastoral vistas.

Gazzrick took them up a wide staircase, carpets of plush wool cushioning each step. The halfling stopped at a balcony that allowed them to overlook a cavernous room. Numerous tables, each flanked by long benches, filled the hall, while servants scurried about to spread white linens and place goblets and platters along the dining surfaces. At the opposite end of the room was a raised dais, with a long table placed where it could overlook the rest of the room. Unlike the other tables, that one had eight tall chairs behind it, obviously reserved for the guests of honor.

"This is the grand throne room and banquet hall," Gazzrick explained. "Normally it's empty, but then you already know this isn't a normal occasion."

"I had noticed," Holt replied. In spite of his determination, however, he couldn't quite muster the glum sense of despair in which he had stubbornly wrapped himself earlier. He had never been here before, and the grandness of the surroundings continued to amaze him.

"Your apartments are down here," Gazzrick explained, leading them into a corridor that branched off the balcony.

"Apartments?" gaped Holt, who had pictured the three of them sharing a small guest chamber.

He was astounded as the halfling ushered them through a high doorway, along a carpeted hall, and into a gracefully appointed sitting room. Four smaller doors led off of this room, and one of these burst open as Derek Jaken rolled out, trailed by two handmaidens.

"Enough with the hair!" shouted the elder Daryman. "My son's here—why don't you pester *him* with your grooming!"

"Father—you look splendid!" Holt declared, amazed at the transformation. An embroidered shirt covered his father's shoulders and torso, and the wheels and struts of his chair had been freshly cleaned and polished. Derek's beard and hair had been trimmed and combed, and it seemed to Holt that the man had an unusual sparkle in his eye.

"Actually, it's kind of fun, being tended by these lovelies," the farmer whispered with a wink. "But watch for those scissors unless you want to feel the sun on the back of your neck next time you go outside!"

Douglas Niles

Indeed, it was a pleasant—and unique—experience for Holt to be groomed and tended by servants. They trimmed his hair and his fingernails, even shaving his sparse whiskers. Finally he thanked them and went into his sleeping chamber. The room was surprisingly huge, with a balcony overlooking the royal gardens. The bed itself was broader by three times than his pallet at home.

Stretched across the quilted surface were black trousers and a white shirt, trimmed in blue. A darker blue mantle, he realized, was to go over the shirt, and after he had donned the full garment he felt rather dashing.

Until he remembered the five guests who would be at the feast. Then his stomach tightened, and he found that he had no appetite for eating with lords and barons and the other assorted 'sirs'. He slumped onto the bed and wondered again how he would ever get a moment to talk with the princess.

How could he have thought of her as a friend? It wasn't Danis's fault, he knew—but when the hall was filled with wealthy, powerful nobles, all vying for her attention and her eye, what chance did he have? He rebuked himself—what kind of ignorant farmboy would even *want* to be in a place like this? He was on the verge of complete despair when he heard a thumping on the door.

"Come on—d'you want to miss the first toast?" demanded the routinely thirsty dwarf.

Holt was on the point of sending the others

down without him, but the refusal caught in his throat. Wearily he stood, drawing some strength from the fact that at the very least he would get to see Danis Vanderthan again—even if it was at a distance.

As he clumped down the stairs, helping Fenrald carry his father's chair while Gazzrick led them on, Holt's spirits lifted slightly. He heard the buzz of conversation from the great hall, the musical laughter of women, the heartier chuckles of men. The sound of clinking glasses chimed from within as they came through the door.

"I *knew* we'd miss that toast!" groused the dwarf.

"Just take two glasses for the next one—that's what I plan to do!" Derek declared, and Holt chuckled slightly.

His poor spirits evaporated completely, then, as Gazzrick led them to their seats. They were close to the royal table, Holt saw, hoping that Danis would be seated near this end. He recognized a familiar figure who stumbled to his feet, knocking over the bench as he fumbled with his spectacles.

"Tut, tut—they need a more solid footing on this thing. But, my boy—is it really you?" asked Tellist Tizzit, scowling suspiciously at the Daryman.

"Tellist! Hello—and of course it's me!"

The wizard squinted determinedly. "Why, dear—yes, I should say that it *is*! At least I *hope* so!"

"It's good to see you!" Holt cried, laughing as he

embraced the flustered old magic-user.

"You've added a pound or two—all muscle, I should say," remarked Tellist, after finally giving his spectacles a proper perch and studying Holt. "But my lad, it's certainly splendid to hear your voice again!"

"It's almost like the trail in the Knollbarrens, we travelers together again," the Daryman declared, overwhelmed by a flush of good feeling.

"Except that the princess and Sir Ira are up on the dais," Tellist pointed out before Gazzrick elbowed him in the ribs.

"And the ale's a good bit colder," Fenrald added, smacking his lips over a tall, frothy mug.

"Lords and ladies—gentlemen and women!" cried a herald. The conversations bubbling throughout the great hall quickly faded. "His Majesty, King Dathwell Vanderthan, will address the gathering."

Trumpets blared, and the monarch, followed by his wife, daughter, and the five contestants, all marched into the room and took their places at the great table. The Daryman was happy to see that the princess was seated at the end nearest him, but dismayed by the fact that her chair was flanked by Prince Gallarath and Baron Durqueson, both of whom shouldered the other aside in an effort to pull out Danis's chair. The princess finally seated herself, while the two fuming noblemen thumped into their own seats, glowering at each other.

Suitors Duel

All of the nobles were dressed in silken finery, bedecked with gems and jewels—though Holt noticed that the Grand Knight of Rockeford restrained himself a little more than the others. He wore shiny leather breeches and tall boots, and even kept his sleek black riding gloves on his hands. Of the five contestants, Sir Erik at least looked like a man of action, not of false poses.

"I extend to you all a welcome and a warm invitation to share our repast. At the same time, I commend to one and all the illustrious heroes who share our table tonight. Each is a man of action and courage; each has demonstrated skill with a weapon; and each holds a high noble station in his own realm.

"Together they represent the lands surrounding Vanderthan, and through our kingdom's long and glorious history, their realms have served as friends, partners—and, it must be admitted—occasionally, enemies. Now they come to us in good health, in the prime of life—er, for the most part," Dathwell noted as the stout Lord Terragal snorted indignantly.

"I ask you all to raise your glasses, to share a toast to our heroes!"

Polite cheers rose from many throats as glasses were raised and drinks quaffed. Holt started to lift his own mug, but couldn't bring himself to make the toast. He was gratified to see that Fenrald, thirsty as he was, also abstained.

Douglas Niles

Dinner consisted of magnificent platters of roasted ox, served with bread, cheese, and an assortment of coastal fruits. Holt, Fenrald, and Derek all acknowledged that they had never had a finer meal, yet the food felt leaden in the Daryman's stomach as King Dathwell rose and prepared to address the crowd.

"Now, each of these men has come here at my invitation," the king continued, "in response to a hitherto mysterious summons that has done no more than mention a contest. Before we explore the details of the affair, I think it behooves us to hear from each of these men. All, as I said, are famed for accomplishment; now, my lords, will you not share the tales of these achievements?"

"Well, normally I try to refrain from such boastful accounts," announced Prince Gallarath, jumping to his feet in the instant before Earl Terrence could stand. The earl sat back down, seething, as the prince began.

"The blue gorgon Terriathia had long been a scourge in Rochester; many a brave knight had met his death seeking to end the creature's grisly career. I, however, perceived a flaw in the plans of my predecessors. . . ."

The prince related, in excruciating detail, the story of his (brilliant) approach to the gorgon's lair, his (heroic) confrontation with the monster, and the (incredibly skillful) fight during which he bested the foe.

Suitors Duel

Immediately afterward, Earl Terrence rose and began to tell the long version of his own tale, the hunt during which he slew the Black Stag. Holt was never quite able to figure out whether the great deer represented some kind of threat or not but, in any event, the earl displayed brilliance, heroism, and skill even surpassing Prince Gallarath's before his tale was concluded.

Baron Durqueson's story culminated in the exceptionally gory death of the bull troll. Since, as Holt had learned, trolls had the unfortunate tendency to heal their hurts and resume the battle, the slaying of the beast was an oft-repeated affair. Each killing, it seemed, required more brilliance, heroism, and skill (and hence more embellishment of the story) than those preceding. Thus the hour had grown quite late by the time the long-winded baron was finished.

Sir Erik politely declined the invitation to speak, announcing that he disdained boastfulness in all its forms. Just when Holt was thinking they approached the end of the speechmaking, however, Lord Bluth Terragal rose and commenced to relate his own heroic tale. It was then that the Daryman remembered: the High Minister of Bedford was famed for the slaying of One Hundred Goblins.

Beginning with the first of these wretched pests, the lord embarked on an epic saga of courage and heroism in the face of overwhelming odds. The gist of the tale involved a treasured goblet that was reputed to be held in a goblin lair. The savage little creatures furiously resisted Lord Terragal's intrusion, and though the noble never did find the goblet, he left in his wake a considerable bit of gore.

Tellist Tizzit nodded off to sleep right around goblin twenty-nine. Fenrald Falwhak made it to some point in the seventies before he, too, was snoring. Holt listened to the whole, lurid saga, alternately fuming and moping over the injustices of life. His only consolation came from an occasional look at Danis, who stirred the remaining food on her plate with an air of complete boredom.

Finally, the lord took a large swig from his mug, wiped his dripping mustache, and concluded: "That big goblin fell right on top of the bodies of his kin. And when I walked out of there, I never looked back!"

For a moment the room was utterly, eerily silent—until Sir Ira, drooping on his perch behind the princess, raised his head and cleared his throat several times. The king looked at the owl expectantly.

"You know, Your Majesty—we are indeed fortunate to be blessed with a plethora of heroes. Men whose brave deeds are exceeded only by their ability to describe those deeds in . . . shall we say 'fascinating and extensive' detail. But I must call to the attention of all that Vanderthan and its environs, such as Oxvale, have also produced men capable of great deeds—though perhaps not so adept at the telling."

"Yes!" cried Danis, delightedly indicating Holt.

The young Daryman flushed, embarrassed, as the owl continued. "I refer, of course, to the Master of the Lodestone Blade, the Slayer of the War-wolf—*and* the Nightshade. Son of Oxvale, he is also the purveyor of the finest cheese in all Kara-wenn. I give you, ladies and gentlemen, Holton Jaken, Daryman of Oxvale!"

"Hurray!" Fenrald had awakened, and now he led the cheering with a lusty yell. Holt's throat tightened as he saw Danis, her face flushed with pride, applauding him.

"Stand up, lad," Derek urged. "Say a few things."

Reluctantly, he pushed back the bench and stood. "I—I'm not a speechmaker, like these grand lords," he said hesitantly. "But, for the notice of my friend Sir Ira, and for the chance to labor in the service of the First Daughter of Vanderthan, I am more grateful than I can say. Thank you."

Now the cheers came from all the gathered folk, and Holt felt a wave of happiness such as he hadn't known since the first suitor had ridden through the palace gates.

"What's this? A cheese-making farmboy has claims to heroism?" demanded Lord Terragal.

"It may come as a surprise to many," King Dath-well interjected, "but the men of Oxvale have been loyal warriors to the crown of Vanderthan for the past four centuries—ever since my ancestors formed this kingdom in an untamed wild. The Darymen have been the Iron Brigade that has formed the backbone of our army on those occasions when we've had to fight. I daresay, Lord Terragal, that you have ancestors in Bedford who would not so readily dismiss the men of Oxvale. Two hundred years ago a company of Darymen routed a full legion of your own troops, at a ford not many miles from here."

"If they have served you so well, then who is lord of this Oxvale? Is there a duke or a baron to lead them? Why is he not present at your court?" Terragal asked insistently.

"Oxvale is known as the Emancipated Common," Gazzrick said helpfully. "It has never had a local lord—yet has been resolute in its service to the king."

"This is unseemly! Perhaps, like so many things, the tales have been exaggerated with the passage of time," declared Baron Durqueson. "Farmers defeating trained knights and warriors. It can't be true!"

"Know, my good baron," the king continued firmly, "that Ironwood, too, has invaded Vanderthan—as recently as the last century. And again it was the Darymen who sent the attackers fleeing home."

Holt's mind was reeling. Never had he heard these tales of his village's prowess. He turned and fixed his father with a penetrating stare, feeling as if a part of his past had been stolen from him by the secrecy. Why had he not been raised to praise this legacy of heroism?

"It is said that the Army of Rockeford, when I was young, was broken by a company of farmers," admitted Sir Erik. He raised a hand, still clad in its black glove, to dissuade Terragal's outrage. "This happened some twenty years hence. These, I assume, were the same warriors?"

"Indeed," King Dathwell agreed, though his face darkened at the memory. "In fact, it is to the heroism of a warrior present in this room that we owe that victory—a man to whom I offered all the riches I could raise as his reward, but who declined payment in order to return to his farm. But that is not the truly remarkable thing about the tale—it is that this humble Daryman, who turned away from a life of luxury and ease, had lost his legs in the battle during which he saved my crown."

Holt whirled back to his father, stunned beyond words. Derek Jaken's face was tight with fury. He looked down at the table, ignoring the pleas from throughout the hall, the calls that he raise his hand, that he make a speech. The younger Daryman was aware of none of this. Holt's feelings were of anguished confusion, soured by a sense of betrayal. Not only had his village's history been concealed from him, but his father had not even shared this crucial part of his own life! Still Derek made no gesture.

It was Lord Terragal who broke the thrall of silence, rising to his feet so rapidly that his chair tumbled to the dais behind him. He fixed Holt and his father with a contemptuous glare. "Why should the deeds of a commoner be given place at a ceremony of lords!"

Holt raised his hand. "Peace," he said. "We mean no—"

"It doesn't matter *what* you mean. The affront itself is enough!"

"What frail shell do you wear that you could take the tale of the Darymen's bravery as an insult?" demanded Fenrald.

"No, r-really—" Holt stammered, embarrassed.

"You seek to back away from the words, farmboy—these *claims* of great deeds?" sneered the lord. Terragal drew back his brown robe, revealing the steel head and sturdy shaft of his mace. "Such arrogance cannot be allowed to pass with a cowardly apology."

"I intend no apology for the acts of my ancestors!" Holt snapped, his temper flaring.

"Then prove the tales with your deeds, boy!" The lord drew his mace and held it up with a flourish. "Meet me on the dueling field! Let's see if the boasts are true—see what kind of battle skill, if any, the farmboy possesses!"

5
To Find A Goat

"Name the time and place—I'll be ready to fight!" Holt shouted, quickly standing. His hand groped for the hilt of the Lodestone Blade as he forgot, momentarily, that he had left his weapon in the palace apartments.

"Holton!" Derek Jaken said, his voice a powerful tug against his son's will. "Sit down!"

The young Daryman flushed, emotions warring within him. A vague part of his mind suggested that he was behaving foolishly, embarrassing his companions and himself. Yet another very loud interior voice demanded in the name of honor that he face the arrogant lord. And deeper still, his confusion at Derek's life of secrets fueled his anger, urging him to ignore his father's words.

Tellist raised his full glass and spoke hesitantly, his words carrying through the tense, still hall. "Perhaps this isn't—oops, tut, tut."

The ceramic mug slipped from the wizard's fingers and shattered on the floor. Immediately red, yellow, and green flames swirled upward from the spilled liquid, leaping from the floor to the table, bouncing like tiny, living creatures across the great hall.

"Oh, dear. We'd best put this out," Tellist declared, stomping on a wisp of flame beside his foot. The flicker danced to the side like a dodging rodent, avoiding the wizard's boot and then scuttling up the edge of the linen tablecloth. It did not appear to singe the cloth, but as it raced along it split into two, then four little blossoms of flame.

Holt saw more fires sweep across the bench behind him and he quickly pounded at them with his hands. He felt no heat under his skin, and the wispy flickers were easily extinguished—without having done any apparent harm to the wooden planks or even the linen tablecloths. Still, the chaotic, bouncing fireballs kept dividing, creating little fire-creatures that careened all about the hall. For several minutes people scrambled madly about, either fleeing the flames or frantically patting and stomping them out. At the head table the contestants and the Vanderthans busily fought the fires.

Finally, gasping for breath, the Daryman stomped out the last of the little flickers. Benches lay strewn about the floor, and many pitchers of water—and a few of good ale, to Fenrald's dismay—had been splashed on the fires.

"Your Majesty, I'm terribly sorry about that," Tellist apologized. "Just a little concoction I've been experimenting with—perhaps it's not quite ready for public display."

"Quite so," agreed the king, though he did not seem terribly displeased. "Now, where were we?

"Oh, yes, to the contest!" The monarch answered himself before Lord Terragal could speak. "Now then, you know that these five nobles have gathered in answer to a challenge. It is time to make this challenge known to one and all!"

The burly lord scowled, flashing Holton a murderous look, but apparently he was intrigued enough by the king's announcement to let the matter drop, for now. The Daryman, however, knew that he had made a formidable enemy.

"Your Majesty—if I may be permitted a word?" Sir Erik—the only suitor who had not boasted of his great deeds—made the polite inquiry.

"What? Oh, well—yes, of course," the king replied.

"Forgive my inelegant intrusion," the Grand Knight of Rockeford said humbly. "But before we learn of the contest, I wonder if I might be permitted to bestow upon the princess a small gift—a token of my high esteem." Before the king could reply Sir Erik drew a small, flat object from within his robe. It was wrapped in white linen, emblazoned with a silken ribbon of green.

"My dear princess," he declared, stepping to Danis's side. "It is my hope that you will accept this gift in the warm spirit with which it is offered. Know that you will see within it the greatest beauty in all Karawenn."

Danis, curious in spite of herself, thanked the knight and untied the ribbon. She pulled the linen away to reveal a small looking glass—when she gazed into it she blushed, obviously remembering the knight's words. "It—it's beautiful," she declared, impressed.

Holt felt another wave of hopeless jealousy. Here was yet one more proof that he didn't belong —could *never* belong—in the exalted company at that high table. Seething, he could only derive a little satisfaction from the glum expressions of the other four suitors. Obviously they had neglected to bring gifts, and now they could only glower at their knightly rival.

"It is known as the Crystal of Seeing," said Sir Erik. "It has hung in the palace of Rockeford for many years; it seemed fitting that it be given a new home. I have heard, though I cannot swear to the truth of it, that when the crystal is spoken to by a person of true faith, it has the power to foretell the future."

Danis, awestruck, looked up at the knight. "How does one know what is the right question to ask?"

"It is a mystery to me. I offer it to you in the sincere hope that, someday, you may unlock its secret."

"Splendid, very nice, wonderful," said the king impatiently. "Now, as to the contest—"

"Beg pardon, my dear," said Tellist, who had somehow made his way to the head table. "I wonder if I might examine that for a moment."

"Of course—but don't drop it," she admonished.

"Tut, tut—I never drop things . . . accidentally," the wizard declared absently, as he sat at the edge of the dais and studied the looking glass.

Realizing that the mage was not about to return to his seat, the king forged boldly ahead. "The contest is in fact a quest—a search that one of these men will complete, returning to Castle Vanderthan with a rare treasure.

"Now, it is a well-known fact that I have but one daughter. As she is coming to a marriageable age, it is only understandable, I think, that I should want her wedding to be the most splendid affair in the history of my—"

"Father!" Danis, her face flushing, rose to her feet. "This is not the—"

"Now, child, humor me. After all, I'm not announcing *whom* you're to marry. I'm simply declaring the terms of the contest to these five brave suitors. And you must realize that your wedding *will* be a grand function—I simply will not have it otherwise. Of course the matter has not been settled yet, but surely you understand that we must, er, narrow the field, so to speak."

Glowering furiously, Danis settled back into her chair. The attention of the five nobles remained fixed unwaveringly on the king. Holt remembered Gazzrick's declaration about this contest, and as he listened to King Dathwell the Daryman knew the halfling had been right—this was a thinly veiled competition to select a husband for the princess.

"Now, as I was saying, for the occasion of your marriage it will be necessary to have the finest of everything to share among our guests—whether this be the roasted meats, the cheeses, the breads and cakes . . . or the wine.

"As a matter of fact, it is to the wine that this contest is directed. Some of you may have heard of the Black Goat of Trollheight?"

The name meant nothing to Holt, but he suspected he would soon learn more.

"She dwells in a high valley of the Trollheight Mountains—a great, proud creature that has never been captured. She is a precious beast because from her udder flows, not milk, but the finest wine in all Karawenn."

"I've heard these legends," growled Lord Terragal. "But who knows if this goat even exists?"

Suitors Duel

"I do." Fenrald Falwhak spoke bluntly. "It's known to the dwarves of Graywall. She was seen, and milked—or wined—by my great-grandfather, as a matter of fact."

"Splendid!" cried the king. "Now, I desire to have this goat—more to the point, the wine from this goat—at my daughter's wedding. The contest will be won by the hero who returns here with the animal!"

"I ride for the Trollheights at first light!" announced Prince Gallarath, sweeping to his feet and raising his clenched fist in the air.

"And I!" Lord Terragal declared.

"I as well!" Earl Terrence was quick to chime in.

"The Black Goat shall be mine!" insisted Baron Durqueson.

"I will devote every fiber of my being to this quest," Sir Erik stated quietly to Danis, after the others had roared their pledges. "This is my word to you, my princess."

"Tut, tut. Oh, dear," said Tellist Tizzit, who, seated before the lords, still stared into the mirror—the mirror that could, maybe, look into the future.

Immediately the great hall fell silent.

"Er, what did you say?" King Dathwell asked hesitantly. "Is it something bad?"

"It's a bit hard to see, actually," the wizard said. "The mirror seems to be a bit smudged." He removed a handkerchief and rubbed at a spot.

"There's—oh, my."

Tellist very gently laid the mirror on the floor and then sidled away from it. The small glass shuddered and trembled, clattering with increasing tempo. Suddenly a gout of green smoke exploded upward, billowing into a thickening column, expanding at the top into a fuming, ominous mushroom shape.

The smoke continued to spew and roil, filling the room with an acrid stench, causing eyes to water. Very slowly, the cloud resolved itself into a humanlike torso, with broad, powerful arms and a leering, dark green face.

The mouth of the murky visage gaped open, while two spots of eyes—utterly, hopelessly black—fixed themselves upon the king of Vanderthan.

"Heed my warning—or the line of Vanderthan shall be extinguished before the year is out!"

The voice was a shuddering, resonant boom that rattled the plates and pressed the awestruck observers back.

"Wha-What do you mean?" stammered the king, trembling before the apparition's glare. Still, the Daryman realized, Dathwell stood and faced the thing, when a lesser man would have been compelled to flee in terror.

"Only in the Trollheight Mountains shall the truth be known!" boomed the smoky messenger. "Only there, in the valley of the Black Goat, shall the blood of Vanderthan be preserved!"

Abruptly a wind swirled loudly through the hall, sweeping hair, fluttering tapestries and linens—and carrying the vestiges of smoke from the air. The billowing cloud reversed its flow, pouring backward into the mirror until every wisp of smoke had disappeared from the room. Finally the wind ceased, and everything settled back into stillness.

"Tut, tut," observed the wizard. "That *was* a bit more than a smudge. I daresay this creates a dilemma."

"Do you believe the prophecy?" asked the king in a horrified whisper. "Does my family stand in danger of perishing before the end of this year?"

"So said the mirror," Sir Erik remembered, his own voice hushed, awestruck. "Unless something occurs in the Trollheights—and princess, I swear that I make haste there immediately, waiting only upon the dawn!"

"You're right," Danis Vanderthan said slowly. "There's great danger to my family—and the mystery might be solved in the valley of the Black Goat."

She turned to the king and planted her hands firmly on her hips. "Father, I must go to the Trollheights as well."

"But, Daughter—"

"Nay, Princess!" Prince Gallarath declared, horrified. " 'Tis not a task for a gentle lady!"

"I'm not so 'gentle' as you might think!" Danis

snapped without taking her eyes from King Dathwell. "I tell you, I'm going!"

"But these men, these suitors—they have the task before them, and they make haste! It would be improper for you to travel with them, so why not wait until they return?"

"Their task is their own, and they may go the way they wish."

"Of course we shall travel as a group—at least, until the objective is near," Earl Terrence declared, with a suspicious look at the others. "But then . . ."

"I shall ask a few old friends to accompany me—if they're willing to take on—"

"My sword is yours, Princess!" Holt declared quietly. His voice nevertheless carried through the room.

"But your suitors are all noblemen—this Daryman, loyal and true though he might be, is hardly of rank with them!"

"Forgive me, Your Majesty," Holt said, firmly clamping down on his outrage. "I do not travel as a suitor—but as a guide, the same service I offered the princess in the Knollbarrens. It may be that she would desire the help of a neutral party, Sire—one who is not involved with the contest. I could provide such aid."

"Graywall's up that way anyway—practically at the foot of the Trollheights," Fenrald said. "I'm on my way back home—mind if I tag along?"

"Thank you, my friends," Danis said, her voice

catching in her throat.

"Tut, tut—I would be remiss if I—"

"No, Tellist—you should stay with Father," the princess gently told the wizard. "He needs you and Gazzrick right now more than ever."

"But—"

"She's right," Holt said, clapping the wizard on the shoulder. "You can keep an eye on that mirror, see if there's anything else you can learn."

"Er, I see—I think," replied the mage, scratching the thin hair stretched across his scalp.

"Enough of this prattling, then," groused Lord Terragal, glowering at the companions. "We ride with the dawn—and we'll be waiting for no woman, dwarf, or farmboy!"

Before Holt could reply, the burly nobleman turned on his heel and stalked from the great hall.

6
A Secret Summons

A dark mood hung around Holt's shoulders, clinging like a sodden cloak as he and Fenrald helped Derek up the stairs to their rooms. His anger still smoldered, flaring up whenever he thought of Lord Terragal—but he recognized that was not the cause of his melancholy.

Perhaps it had been that smoky apparition. The sense of menace and terror in its presence had been pronounced, overpowering. But neither was that what weighed his spirits down.

Derek sat silently as they reached the top of the

stairs. Holt started to push the chair, but his father instead took the wheels and propelled himself away, apparently understanding his son's mood.

And Derek knew that he, himself, was the cause.

"I'm not so tired—think I'll walk around a bit, stretch my legs and work off the meal," Fenrald muttered awkwardly as they reached the door. "You two go ahead." The dwarf clumped, with exaggerated casualness, down the castle corridor.

After he closed the door Holt turned grimly to his father. An explosion of questions and accusations surged upward. The Daryman's sense of shock finally fell away and the fullness of betrayal came to the surface.

"*Why?* Why did you keep everything such a secret from me? It's my life, my home—and you haven't told me a single thing about it! About a glorious past! A legacy of honor and heroism!"

"And a price . . . a price of blood and flesh," Derek sighed. "Perhaps it was wrong—but perhaps not. It was a thing I chose not to discuss."

"Not just you," Holt declared. "None of our neighbors spoke of it, either. I've spent long days listening to Nowell the Aching complain, or tell his long-winded tales—not *once* did he speak of the sacrifices, the bold deeds of the Darymen! At the very least, I should have known about the pledge made by the men of Oxvale to the king of Vanderthan!"

"That pledge is no longer in effect!" Derek snapped. "And it has no bearing on your life!" The farmer's tone grew softer, more wistful as he continued. "Though it seems there are destinies powerful enough to override an old man's efforts. Even with no knowledge of the pledge, you once undertook a valiant quest in the name of the House of Vanderthan. And now, it seems, you will begin another."

"Yes—and this makes it more right than ever. But how can you declare null a pledge that has stood for four centuries?"

"It was the Troll War, my son—that was the final measure of Oxvale's loyalty. At the cost of my legs, and the lives of too many good men who should have been your neighbors, and whose sons should have been your friends."

"But is that not the cost of war? And was not the Troll War just?"

"Aye, son—just and necessary, unless we wanted warwolves and trolls to rule the land. But it was a struggle that lasted for fifteen years, and during the darkest phase, it came to the very fields of Oxvale itself. . . ." Derek's eyes misted and he drew a deep and ragged breath.

"The Winter of Tears," Holt whispered. "When my mother died, when so many died of hunger."

"There, too, you have not heard the truth. It was *not* hunger that killed so many Daryfolk," Derek said fiercely. "It was trolls! The Iron Brigade was gone, leading the king's army in a campaign that never found an enemy! Only two warriors remained in the village—myself, for I had been wounded the year before, and Nowell son of Nowscon. Nowell was the defender of the village, a mighty warrior who bore the Lodestone Blade with skill. He remained there by custom—for the sword was rarely taken from Oxvale, and one man always remained behind as guardian and champion of the families."

"Nowell . . . a *warrior?*" The chronically complaining old man was the least warlike fellow Holt could imagine.

His father continued as if he hadn't heard the interruption. "The trolls came on a misty dawn . . . they were already among the houses by the time we saw them. Nowell killed many, but in the end they bore him to ground, smashing his arms and legs and laughing at his helplessness and suffering.

"And as to helplessness," Derek said, his voice filled with loathing, "there was *me!* Sitting in my chair—I shot arrows until they took my weapon away . . . they dragged me into the street . . . left me beside Nowell while they laughed, and—"

The Daryman dropped his head into his hands, unable to continue. Holt sat back, too stunned to say anything. He despised himself for challenging his father, for bringing these memories to the fore.

"At least your mother managed to hide you . . . she put you under the bed and you stayed quiet there—three months old, and you didn't let out a cry. And a few others survived—Merry Biddlesome, the one you call 'Hag' now—hid with the little Wainwright girls in a haystack. The trolls never looked there."

"Father, please—I'm sorry," Holt said, finally clasping the man in his arms. His mind reeled with horrific images, but he no longer wanted to hear. Still, Derek Jaken continued, speaking as much to himself as to his son.

"There was a man with the trolls, a young fighter, who led them. Nowell faced him—he cut the man's hand with the Lodestone Blade, chopping off some of his fingers. But then the trolls dragged Nowell down, and this captain—this *monster*—ordered the beasts to break Nowell's bones! Then he ordered the trolls to search the village, to burn everything. I have never seen a man so cruel."

Derek sat up, clearing his throat firmly and blinking back his tears. "The war dragged on for two more years. Most of the Darymen perished, though a few came back—Karl Fisher, the Wilbert Brothers, Young Miller. . . .

"But the brigade was gone, really. And again we Darymen had won for Vanderthan a war. But we all agreed that it was the last time . . . we sent the king a compact and told him this."

"And what happened?"

"We never heard from the crown of Vanderthan again," Derek replied. "And so, until your adventure in the Knollbarrens, I had thought that our ties were fully severed. We would be a village of farmers and cheese-makers, and be happy with the bounty of our lands—and for the lives of those of us who still breathed."

"And the Lodestone Blade . . . ?" Holt's thoughts turned to the weapon that Nowell and his father had bestowed upon him before his trip into the Knollbarrens. "It belongs to Oxvale?"

"It has always been borne by a Daryman—sometimes with skill, on other occasions with luck. But since our ancestor chipped it from the Source Lodestone centuries ago, it has never broken."

"Why didn't the trolls take it after they . . . after Nowell was . . . ?"

"They feared it. He'd killed a dozen of them with it, and it frightened them. There's a thing about trolls—like that too-handsome baron said. You can cut them with a weapon, and the wound'll close right up, whole as new. Cut off an arm, it crawls back to the body and latches on to the stump—it's the most grotesque thing I've ever seen."

Holt shuddered, imagining the gruesome regeneration as his father continued.

"But the Lodestone Blade—when it cut them, they *stayed* cut. Guess they figured it would be a menace to have around. Anyway, none of them even wanted to pick it up."

The younger Daryman rose and crossed to the sword, where it hung in its leather scabbard from a peg in the wall. He drew the blade, which shed a soft, rosy light across the darkened room.

"It never glowed like that," said Derek. "Not until you touched it to the Source Lodestone. Though old tales said it was glowing when it was first made—and stayed that way for several generations.

A gentle tapping on the door caught Holt's attention. "Fenrald?" he asked, wondering if their companion had returned. The tapping was repeated, with no other reply.

The Daryman sheathed his sword and crossed to the portal. "Yes?" he inquired, surprised to see a palace attendant, in a gleaming satin uniform, standing there.

"Good evening, sir. I have been requested to give you this." The fellow extended a thin page, rolled into a scroll and wrapped with a red ribbon.

Puzzled, Holt mumbled his thanks as he took the scroll and closed the door. Unrolling it, he returned to his father.

"Getting some mail?" asked the elder Jaken, trying to lighten the mood.

"It's a short message—'Please meet me beside the garden pool, as soon as possible.' It's signed with a 'D.'"

"Best not to keep a lady waiting," Derek said with a twinkle in his eye. "I'm going to bed, so take your time about it."

His heart bouncing, Holt made his way through the quiet corridors of the castle, down the stairs into the great hall. A few servants labored there, cleaning up the mess of the feast, but they paid him no attention as he skirted the hall and left by the side doors—which he had guessed would take him into the garden.

He crossed a wide patio, moving by the light of bright stars and a sliver of moon, until he reached the tall hedges surrounding the pool. He felt fairly certain he could remember his way through the maze—and besides, the garden wasn't *that* big.

His memory served him well: he passed around several corners and followed a long aisle before entering the large, circular clearing around the pool. The marble statues glowed with a pearly light, seeming to pick up every trace of the natural illumination. The surrounding hedges and lawn, by contrast, were murky with shadow, and the pond itself might have been a great pool of ink.

Holt took a few steps forward, passing several alabaster pedestals bearing busts of Vanderthan ancestors. He wondered about the lack of light. Wouldn't Danis have brought a lantern with her? Abruptly his skin prickled with a sense of acute anxiety. He turned quickly, but saw nothing.

Yet when he turned back to the water he got the distinct impression, in the corner of his eye, that one of the statues had moved. A great, rearing horse, carved with snorting nostrils and flaring mane, bearing a warlike knight, stood between him and the pond.

Advancing cautiously, the Daryman looked to the right and the left, growing more and more certain of a dark suspicion: Danis Vanderthan had had nothing to do with the summons he had received.

The attacker lunged from behind the statue of the horseman. Cold steel gleamed in the starlight, a dagger in a fist that lashed toward Holt's face. In a flicker the Daryman pictured his sword, hanging from a peg on the wall of his chamber.

Then his instincts took over. The shadowy knifeman was huge, charging Holt like a maddened bear. As that wicked blade hooked forward the Daryman raised his arm in a desperate parry, feeling the knife cut his wrist even as he blocked it from his face.

Gritting his teeth against the pain, Holt stumbled backward, then darted to the side. The hulking attacker lunged after him, but the Daryman planted his feet, then kicked sharply as the man came close. His foot caught the attacker in the knee, and with a grunt of rage the fellow stumbled and fell.

Spinning on his heel, Holt darted toward the gap in the hedge, but with surprising agility the man groped across the ground and tripped him. Crawling now, the Daryman looked back to see the shadowy form rise to its feet. Again that blade picked up the faint illumination of the night sky, glimmering against the blackness.

78

Holt bounded to his feet, dodging between a pair of small statues as the knife-man slashed after him. Knocking against a stony visage, the Daryman dived away, desperately crawling beneath the belly of the rearing horse. Though he limped from the effects of Holt's kick, the attacker nevertheless came around the statue with grim perseverance.

Frantically the young farmer dashed into the maze, hearing his pursuer thudding behind. Holt cut to the right, then left, darting between the high banks of greenery. But now there was a strangeness to the aisles, and as he whirled around another intersection he knew that, somehow and somewhere, he'd taken a wrong turn.

One more intersection sent the Daryman crashing into a barrier of hedge, and as he frantically turned to the right and left he saw that he'd entered a narrow cul-de-sac. He spun about, placing his back to the hedge, and faced the looming figure and his deadly steel blade.

"Who are you?" Holt demanded. "Why are you doing this?"

"Who?" The fellow laughed cruelly, and there was a familiar, gloating arrogance in the sound. "Someone you'll never humiliate again, farmboy!"

"The guard—at the gatehouse," the Daryman said, his voice level—though his heart pounded in near panic.

"That's me," sneered the man, still chuckling. "And as to the why—well, it's good for a man to die with a question on his lips."

With shocking speed the guard thrust the knife, but Holt saw the flash of motion in the dark. He met the blow with both hands, seizing the wrist of the man's knife-hand, trying to hold that keen edge away from his throat. Yet the brute was huge and powerful. Slowly, his strength pressed the weapon downward.

Prickly branches dug into his back, but the Daryman was only dimly aware of the pain. Sweat beaded across his forehead, and the tendons in Holt's arms stretched taut as bowstrings, desperately trying to delay disaster. But even all of his strength was insufficient to hold the burly guardsman at bay. Holt pressed backward into the hedge, ignoring the cuts in his skin. The knife wound in his arm throbbed, and he felt his strength ebbing.

With a burst of energy, the guardsman heaved, grunting from the exertion, driving that deadly blade even closer. Frantically Holt pushed to the side, and gaped in surprise as the fellow tumbled in response to the Daryman's shove. With a deep, exhausted groan, the man flopped onto his belly, twitching on the ground for a moment before lying still.

Vaguely Holt made out the hilt of another knife—this one buried in the treacherous guardsman's back. A shadowy figure leaned close, checking the attacker for a pulse before straightening up. All the Daryman could see was a silhouette in the darkness.

"Thank you," Holt gasped, straining to pull air into his lungs. He felt drained of all energy, all emotion—except for a dull sense of shock, surprised that he was still alive. "You saved my life."

"Think nothing of it—the pleasure, and honor, are mine."

Stunned, Holt could not believe his ears. Yet as he squinted and looked closer, he saw that he had not made a mistake.

His rescuer was the elven thief, Syssal Kipican.

7
A Night Stroll

"What are you doing here?" Holt demanded, trying to settle his breathing to a more normal level. "The guards said you must have gone over the wall, made your escape!"

"They were right on one account," the elf said, a droll smile flashing his teeth in the darkness. "I did make my escape, but I was enjoying the castle so much that I decided to postpone my departure for a few hours."

"Enjoying . . . ? But they were looking for you all over the place! If someone saw you—"

"I should say I was seen. After all, it would have

been hard to attend the feast without getting noticed," Syssal remarked. "And it would have been a shame to miss that splendid repast. We elves have never learned to roast meat as well as you humans."

"But—you were at the *feast?*" Holt blurted.

"In disguise, of course," the elf explained. "Darken my hair, alter the color of my cloak, and I look like any of a hundred courtiers or dandies who were taking advantage of the free food."

"The bracelet!" Holt remembered. "How did you get it away from me?"

"Now, don't get ideas about taking it back," the elf warned. "I told you, it's the property of my family. As for how, do you remember when I bumped against you as we came around a corner in the hedge? You have a most inadequate buckle on your belt pouch."

"You know, I *have* to trust you," the Daryman said, shaking his head in amazement. "After all, why would a guilty man risk his life to save the one who apprehended him?"

"Good point—I'm glad you have the cleverness to observe it. But, for the record, I think it would be best if I went over the wall now. It's been a splendid visit, but I daresay that I should be moving on. I'm glad we had the chance to speak on a less, er, adversarial basis."

"Agreed," Holt said. "I've never met an elf before —you've given me good cause to think fondly of your people."

They heard the footsteps of several men as the light of flickering torches glimmered over one of the nearby hedges. "Is anyone here?" demanded a gruff voice. "Show yourself—in the name of the king!"

"My cue," whispered Syssal, who ducked low and vanished into the shadows at the base of the hedge. Looking after him, Holt couldn't see a single trace of where the elf had gone.

"Who's there? Speak up!" demanded the searcher, again.

"Over here," Holt said, after insuring that Syssal was nowhere to be seen. "It's me—Holton Jaken. I've been attacked."

"What's that? Who attacked you?" growled a suspicious voice—none other than King Vanderthan himself.

Several guardsmen, swords drawn and torches held high, came around a corner of the hedge, followed quickly by the monarch. Holt faced them over the body of the murderous captain. The Daryman realized with vague shock that it was his own knife—the one he had lost at the same time as the bracelet—that struck the killing blow.

"What happened?" asked the king, bluntly surveying the scene.

As briefly as possibly, Holt related the events beginning with his receipt of the summons. He omitted any mention of Syssal Kipican, claiming that he had forgotten until the last minute that he had his knife in his belt. All the time that he spoke, King Dathwell stood listening, no flicker of emotion showing on his face.

"That bears out what Jakobb—the messenger who brought you the note—said. He claimed Tullow gave him the note and a gold piece to deliver it without saying anything to anyone." The king indicated the dead man. "Of course, Jakobb didn't read the note—but he became suspicious when Tullow disappeared from his post. Then he came to warn me."

"I'm glad he did," Holt said sincerely.

"Why would Tullow want to kill you?" the ruler asked finally.

"I don't know. He tried to bully us at the gate this afternoon and perhaps I showed him up a bit—but that's hardly cause for murder!"

"Well, it's a relief to see that you escaped without harm—and a certain tribute to yourself. Tullow was famed for his skill with the knife. You're fortunate to be alive."

"That I am," Holt murmured with silent thanks to the valiant elf.

"Take care of the remains," King Dathwell ordered his men. "The scoundrel is to have a traitor's burial, on the other side of the river." He turned back to Holt. "Take one of these torches and walk with me—I would speak to you for a moment."

"Certainly, Your Majesty." The Daryman did as

he was told, walking beside the king as Dathwell wandered through the maze. The monarch's head was lowered, his brow creased in thought. Finally he stopped and turned to Holton.

"Now see here," he began awkwardly. "I want it understood that I recognize your service to my daughter. She, Gazzrick, and Tellist have made it quite clear that, without your presence, she would almost certainly have perished on the quest for the crown. Nor do I wish to imply that your motives were other than altruistic and honorable."

Mystified, the Daryman could only nod cautiously.

"By the same token—now that she has taken this idiotic notion of traveling to the Trollheight Mountains—it is somewhat of a relief that she has commissioned you as her guide."

"The honor is mine," Holt said truthfully.

"Yes, er—I imagine it is. Now, then. The crux of the matter. The issue we need to discuss. The, um . . ."

Taken aback by the monarch's obvious discomfort, Holt blurted: "Is it about the suitors?"

The king sighed in relief. "Yes, I want there to be no misunderstandings regarding rank and station. After all, it is my hope and intention that one of these men will become the next king of Vanderthan. I will not allow any misperceptions on their part regarding the affections my daughter holds for you. You are a friend, a bold protector—this I grant. You must make certain that this is where it remains."

"I understand, Your Majesty," Holt said, again keeping his fury under control. What cruel joy these nobles must take, he thought bitterly, each time one of them reminds me of my low station. "Your daughter is safe with—and *from*—me."

"That's not what I meant," snapped the king, fixing Holt with an iron glare that reminded the Daryman that he faced a monarch who had ruled his realm for three decades, surviving war and prospering during peace.

"I—I realize that. I am sorry, Sire."

They had passed beyond the gardens of the hedge to approach a side door to the keep. Beyond, a lamplit corridor extended toward the great hall.

"This quest—it is something to which I have devoted a great deal of thought. It is important, when you enter the mountains, that the suitors seek the goat without aid or interference from you or Danis."

"Forgive me, Sire, but what does the search for a wine-giving goat reveal about a man's virtues, either for royalty or as a husband?" Holt had wondered a great deal about the odd choice of contest.

"More about the former than the latter, I should say—and a kingship, after all, is what's at stake here. The contest will reveal tenacity, ruthlessness, and intelligence about the suitors. The real reason, however, is a dream I had one night: that I stood before the next king of Vanderthan, and he gave me this goat as a present."

They came around a corner below the great staircase and saw Sir Erik Merriwell approaching. The knight was clad in green silk, and now he paced absently toward them, his hands behind his back. Abruptly he stopped. "Your Majesty! It is a pleasure to see you. I had difficulty sleeping, and decided to go for a stroll about your magnificent keep."

"It is splendid, is it not?" the king declared, stepping beside the knight and leaving Holt a couple paces behind. "Do you know that the white quartz was mined in the Knollbarrens and carted here at great expense?"

"Fascinating."

Holt was ready to go back to his chambers and sleep, but he sensed that one wasn't supposed to just walk away from the king. So he tromped miserably along, listening to the pair exchange compliments and boasts about the castle.

"Your own quarters, you've seen, are paneled in dark mahogany from the seacoast," the king continued as they came up the stairway to the intersection of second-floor corridors.

"Quite remarkable," Sir Erik agreed. "Now this, to the left, seems a much lighter wood. A different source, no doubt?"

"Different and newer," the king agreed with a

pleased nod. "This hallway, leading to the guest quarters of Baron Durqueson and Prince Gallarath, is walled in white oak. It was installed barely twenty years ago, during my reign."

"Excellent selection," the knight replied with apparently sincere appreciation. "Your woodworkers have done—" Sir Erik ceased speaking, raising a hand to his ear.

"What is it?" asked the king in a whisper. "Did you hear something?"

They all heard it this time—a gasp of surprise, mingled with fear. In another instant the hallway rang with a piercing female scream.

"What's going on?" shouted the king. "Who is that? What's the matter?"

"In here!" Holt cried, springing to one of the doors along the hallway. Pressing his ear to the portal he heard something heavy fall over, followed by another grunt. "There's a fight or something in this room!"

"Those're Baron Durqueson's quarters," the king objected. "How dare—"

"He's right, Your Majesty," declared Erik, who had joined Holt at the door.

"What's that? Open up in there! I demand you open this door—in the name of the king!" cried Dathwell, thumping a solid fist against the sturdy oaken planks.

"Stand aside, Sire." Sir Erik stepped back, lowering his shoulder toward the door. Holt had felt the portal, and it seemed plenty solid to him, but he admired the knight's determination.

Hurling himself forward, Sir Erik smashed into the door and carried the barrier inward with the force of his onslaught. The knight tumbled to the floor but quickly sprang to his feet as Holt and the king crowded in behind them.

The Daryman had to suppress an immediate urge to laugh out loud.

Baron Durqueson of Ironwood, suitor to the First Daughter of Vanderthan, had quite obviously been chasing a servant maiden around the room. The girl, clutching her tattered dress about her, stared in shock and awe at the king.

"Sire!" she wailed, collapsing to the floor in a huddle of sobbing misery.

"You scoundrel!" snapped King Dathwell, confronting the baron furiously.

"Bu-But, Your Majesty! The wench came to me uninvited! She teased and cavorted—and only in the last moment did she begin to scream and throw things! I have been most foully betrayed!"

"Betrayed, perhaps—but the foulness is all your own!" growled the monarch. His face flushed so red that the color glowed crimson through the white hair of his beard.

"You will depart this castle now, immediately! You have one hour—and if I find you here after that time, your next stop will be my dungeon! Do I make myself understood?"

Douglas Niles

The baron did not reply—but he did begin grabbing articles of clothing strewn about the room, frantically throwing them into a voluminous bag.

"You will go to the housekeeper and make your explanation," the king said to the girl, who had begun to recover her composure. Nodding abjectly, she scuttled toward the door.

As King Dathwell and Sir Erik continued to observe the baron, Holt turned and saw the girl tuck something into a boot by the door. The Daryman sauntered over and looked down to see a small key—suitable in size at least, to fit the lock on the door of this room.

Thoughtfully, he looked at the door. The force of Sir Erik's blow had knocked the lock out of the wall, but the bar that could be used to further secure the portal was barely scratched. Examining the bracket on the doorframe, he noticed that a handkerchief had been wadded up and pressed into the frame, so that the bar could not be lowered more than a fraction of an inch into its notch.

"Your Majesty . . . ?"

"What? Oh, that's all I wanted to talk you about —why don't you get back to your quarters?" With the brusque suggestion, the monarch turned back to glower at Durqueson.

Flushing, Holt bowed stiffly and stepped through the door. Already forgotten by the occupants, the Daryman stalked down the hall, still hearing the voices from the room.

Suitors Duel

The baron continued to proclaim his innocence, but the king was believing none of it. At last Durqueson hoisted his bag and marched to the door.

"I tell you, I've been betrayed!" he declared. "And you're making a mistake by sending me away! It's a mistake you'll all regret!"

Leaving his vague threat ringing in the air, the Baron of Ironwood turned and marched away.

8
The Tannyv Trail

The party prepared for the road, as the noblemen had sworn, by first light. Holt got Old Thunder saddled and ready, while Danis prepared
Lancer, her fleet charger. The princess had found a
stocky, short-legged pony to carry Fenrald.

Tellist, the king, and Derek joined the travelers
in the stable while the four noble suitors went to
see to their own steeds.

"His Majesty has invited me to stay here until
you return," the elder Daryman told his son with a
chuckle. "I'm guessing that I'll be more comfortable than you will."

"I hope so—but Old Thunder's back is fine for me," Holt replied. He'd mentally compared his big horse to the steeds the nobles had ridden. While Thunder was not so sleek, nor probably as fast as the other mounts, he was easily the largest of their horses, and no doubt the strongest. The Daryman felt no regrets about facing the adventure mounted on his steady old companion.

"Tut, tut," said Tellist, blinking in concern as he stood beside the princess. "You'd all best be careful—*very* careful. Er, I have a small favor to ask. Here's a wineskin—when you find that goat, would you be so terribly kind as to fill it for me? I'd be very grateful!" He handed Danis a supple leather sack, neatly decorated with a pattern of gold and silver beads.

"Sure, Tellist—we will. And we will be careful, I promise," replied the young woman.

"And I'll be there to keep an eye on things," declared Sir Ira, settling to a perch on the hitching post. "No doubt I'll be steering you away from all manner of trouble!"

Holt laughed, but was nevertheless glad to know that the wise old bird would be flying along.

When the four nobles mounted their own chargers the party made its final farewells. The castle gates were open, and soon the seven riders were on their way, Sir Ira winging into the sky overhead. With minimal talking they rode through the quiet streets, out the city gates and along the smooth track that followed the course of the River Tannyv.

It was a good day for such a ride, Holt reflected. The sky was clear, the air crisp and dry. The first tinges of autumn color had given way to a full glory of reds, oranges, and golds, sparkling in the sunshine across the many groves of oaks, maples, hickories, and other hardwoods.

Unlike the narrower track to Oxvale, on the other side of the river, this was a well-traveled road. Often the party met individual farmers or merchants carting goods to Vanderton, or passed groups of school children or shepherds and their flocks. No matter who they met, the other party always gave way to the proud, prancing warhorses of the four lords.

After enduring castle, nobles, elegant halls, and good manners, Holt found the saddle a comfortable and familiar vantage, as soothing in its way as the healing spell Sir Ira had cast upon the knife wound in his arm the night before. Remembering that the owl's enchantments had saved Holt's life, Holt had sought the owl and asked him to perform the curing magic on the deep gash. This time, Sir Ira had muttered an incantation and brushed his feathers across the wound, causing the cut to vanish entirely. Holt was left profoundly grateful for the deep and ancient power abiding in the mysterious old owl.

Now the Daryman was glad for Sir Ira's presence on the journey. Once beyond the city walls, the bird settled to Danis's shoulder, then hopped down to the horn of her saddle. Holt held Old Thunder back from the princess for the first part of the ride, preferring to ride in relaxed silence beside Fenrald.

Though the number of suitors had been reduced by one, four noblemen seemed like more than enough as far as the Daryman was concerned. Three of them—Prince Gallarath, Lord Terragal, and Earl Terrence—constantly pestered the princess with their attentions. Occasionally Holt rode close enough to hear them talk, but he quickly got an earful of tepid flatteries and pompous boasts.

Of the suitors, only Sir Erik did not force his attentions on Danis, but like Holt waited until she had a word for him. Perhaps because he did not rank as highly as the others, the Grand Knight of Rockeford spent a lot of time riding by himself, lost in thought. Also unlike the others, the knight continually wore his gleaming black armor—the finest suit of mail Holt had ever seen. And even when he took a drink of water or wiped the dust from his face, he never removed his shiny black gloves.

Once, when Prince Gallarath and Lord Terragal had Danis bracketed, each lord trying to outdo the boasts of the other, Sir Ira flipped into the air, spiraled lazily a few times, and settled onto Holt's saddle.

"Speaking as one who is not lacking in self-confidence," the owl declared with a sigh, "I have never before encountered two such tiresomely boastful windbags!"

"How long do we have to listen to them?" Holt wondered ruefully. "I don't even know how far it is to the Trollheight Mountains."

"I should say four or five days' travel ought to bring us to the foothills," Sir Ira observed. "The river forms the border of Amana for part of its length there, and then swings inward to the flatland country of Rockeford. In the uplands to the other side of the stream lies the frontier of Rochester—Prince Gallarath's realm."

"Five *days?*" Holt was used to shorter distances, and only now did he realize that he'd be journeying farther from home than ever before. Still, it was not the distance that caused him distress—it was the unavoidable presence of his traveling companions.

Old Thunder clopped along, gradually catching up to the listless pace of Earl Terrence's charger. The thin-faced young nobleman looked at Holt with disinterest as the Daryman pulled beside him. Terrence quickly turned his attention to the backs of Terragal and Gallarath, who still flanked the First Daughter of Vanderthan.

"In Amana I travel about in a carriage—a *golden* carriage," declared the earl. "It makes a far more comfortable arrangement than this saddle."

Holt studied the man. After half a day on the trail, Earl Terrence already looked ragged and wan. His carefully sculpted hair had fallen in limp ringlets, and a layer of dust had collected across his sweat-streaked brow. The earl's silken garments sagged, clinging to his thin shoulders and narrow chest, outlining a physique that seemed to verge on the sickly. The crossbow that was his favored weapon was tied carelessly to his horse's withers—Holt guessed that the man would need several minutes to unlash and cock it.

The Daryman remembered his first sight of Earl Terrence, when the elegant nobleman had disdainfully flicked away the traces of dust that touched his boots and leggings. Now, it seemed, the fellow was too tired even to notice his disheveled state.

"You, there—farmboy!" The bellow from ahead drew Holt's attention like the flash of menacing lightning. He scowled as he saw Lord Terragal gesturing him forward with a commanding wave.

Grimly, the Daryman chose to ignore the summons, drawing some satisfaction from the sight of Danis rebuking the burly nobleman. He couldn't hear what she said, but he saw Terragal slouch sullenly in his saddle. The trio in the lead came to a halt, and allowed Terrence and Holton to catch up; Fenrald, in the rear, came along at an easy walk.

"We'll stop for a meal here," Terragal declared, gesturing to an open meadow just off the road. "Build us a fire," he ordered Holt.

The Daryman was about to snap back, telling the lord to build his own fire, when Danis spoke. "We don't need a fire—let's make this a short rest. And when we do need coals for cooking, or a lean-to, we'll *all* do the work. There are no masters and no servants on the trail."

"Aye, there's a brave lad," said Terragal scornfully. "To let a woman make yer arguments for you."

"No one needs to do my speaking for me," Holt said. "And no one needs to make your fire, either."

"The lad's right," said Prince Gallarath, with a gallant smile for the princess. "The march to adventure brings out the heart of any man—it makes us equal in our skills and our fortunes. Equal in everything, for that matter, except in the matter of birth."

With this assertion, the prince dismounted and set about finding some clover for his horse. Holt broke out a block of cheese, sharing it with Danis and, grudgingly, the noblemen. He was relieved when the short rest came to an end, and they mounted and started again along the road.

By late afternoon they came to a shady inn at a remote junction of roads called Mossbridge. Here the princess made arrangements for rooms. When the innkeeper had insufficient space, Holt was actually relieved that Fenrald suggested he and the Daryman could stay in the stable. The discomforts of a night among the horses would pale by

comparison to the relief they got, well-removed
from the boasting and bragging of their companions. Sir Ira, too, found dry and comfortable shelter
on a hitching post beside the pair.

The next morning, too, they made an early start
—though Prince Gallarath had to haul the protest-
ing Earl Terrence out of bed. Still, the party was on
the road within an hour after dawn, and for another day of good weather they advanced steadily
up the valley of the great river.

The companions gradually moved into the highlands. The colors of the leaves grew richer and
more vivid until the road became an aisle bordered
by shimmering hues too bright for any mortal-
made dye. Because the forest remained so thick,
they saw little of the bluffs and heights that closed
in on the great valley. An occasional mountainous
summit, rounded and crowned by trees, showed
through the forest ahead of them. Sir Ira, when he
dropped in, described the upward slope of the land.
The owl spent more and more time in air, however,
expressing his growing disgust for the arrogant
nobles when he rested for a short stint on the
Daryman's saddle.

Holt saw the changes in the landscape expressed
mostly in the river. Imperceptible mile by mile, yet
obvious by the end of a few hours, the Tannyv continued to narrow and the speed of the current
increased. By the end of the third day the great
waterway roiled and rumbled along, far too fast to

ford or ferry. Waters that became brown, muddy with silt in the lower stretches now rippled and flashed, surging over a rocky bed that lay clearly revealed. Often Holt saw trout jumping, and wished that he had the luxury to stop and fish. Indeed, when the boasting of the lords became especially tiresome, he even toyed with the idea of abandoning the quest and sitting beside this magnificent waterway.

It was only the presence of Danis Vanderthan that kept him with the group. For days, he subsisted on her quick word or occasional, flashing smile—directed at him. Whether he and Fenrald slept in stables or guest rooms, they didn't mix with the nobles during their nightly stops. Fortunately, Danis retired early each evening, leaving the lords with little to do but go to bed.

They awakened on the sixth morning to see that clouds had rolled in during the night, and a dank, penetrating mist clung to the boles of the trees, wisping among the now dull-looking foliage. Again Earl Terrence didn't want to rise, and Terragal was none too gentle in dumping the young dandy out of bed.

They set out on the road in their usual order, though for the first time on the journey Sir Ira had flown away before the dawn. In the past the owl had sometimes soared for great distances, so neither Holt nor Danis was concerned by the fact that he was nowhere to be seen. The lords, conversely, were delighted to do without him.

Immediately after they rode away from the inn, the road began a sharp series of curves, ascending a steep, rocky bluff that reared close beside the river's bank. After several of these tight turns, Holt looked down to see the inn, almost swallowed by the mist, hundreds of feet below them. A steep precipice plunged away directly at the side of the road.

On this narrow, steep route Earl Terrence and Sir Erik flanked Danis, while Prince Gallarath and Lord Terragal rode forward to scout the rest of the road. As the group reached the steepest stretch of the climb, the pair, their reconnaissance completed, came loping back.

The bullying Terragal pulled his horse to halt before Sir Erik, who rode beside the steep drop-off. The blocking tactic was one Holt had seen the lord use several times before. The knight paused, allowing the lord to draw even with Princess Danis.

This time, however, something seemed to startle Terragal's horse. The big charger reared in panic, hooves slipping on the steep, muddy road. With a shrill cry of terror the animal slid over the lip of the embankment. Terragal barely hurled himself to safety before the steed tumbled piteously onto the rocks below.

Cursing and blustering, the lord climbed to his feet and dusted himself off. Prince Gallarath pulled him to safety while the others drew up and dismounted.

"Are you all right?" Danis asked the lord.

"Aye—but without a steed! The fool beast should have known better than to rise up like that!"

"Looks like he won't be doing it anymore," Holt declared with a grim look at the dead horse. He wondered if he felt worse than he would have if the nobleman himself had fallen—and he wasn't sure he wanted to know the answer.

"That was a foolish risk you took." Danis declared. "And it's a shame that poor beast had to pay the price."

The lord flushed, but made no reply.

"We can't hold up for one on foot, old fellow," Prince Gallarath said breezily. "Do you want to walk along behind, or wait here while I go and fetch the goat?"

"No—I'll ride," Terragal said grimly, his scowl so dark that his skin glowed red. He gestured past Holt, to Old Thunder. "I'll take the farmboy's horse. True, it's no beauty, but it's big and strong enough to carry me. The lad can get himself another when he finds a horse-trader."

Holt objected loudly as Terragal reached past him to seize the big horse's bridle. Before the Daryman could draw his sword, however, Thunder reared and kicked a big, shaggy forehoof, driving the foot into Lord Terragal's leg.

The sound of breaking bone was quickly outdone by the nobleman's bellow of pain. Terragal collapsed, grasping his thigh, while Holt seized

Old Thunder's reins and brought the big horse under control.

A moan drew their attention as Earl Terrence—his horrified eyes fastened on the jagged angle of Terragal's leg—wobbled to the side and then fainted, falling into the muddy road with a splash.

"Our earl seems to be a squeamish one. I presume he slew the Black Stag without bloodshed," Sir Erik remarked wryly, drawing a tight smile from Danis.

"The owl!" moaned Lord Terragal. "That beast can heal me—I saw him mend the farmboy's arm! Where is the accursed featherbag?"

But Sir Ira was nowhere to be found. In the end they were forced to make a litter and return Lord Terragal to the inn below the bluff. There he would be well tended, at least until he could travel again.

Later in the morning, as they rode back up the hill, following the long river valley, Holt found it hard not to smile.

9
The Coming
of Cold

The first night the companions spent out of doors was also the first night it snowed. Heavy, wet flakes settled quietly around them, beginning just before sunset. In the early darkness the wind picked up, slipping through the trees with a hissing, raspy sound. As the temperature dropped the snow grew more fine, whipping against their exposed skin with stinging prickles.

Holt located a sheltered hollow where dense, overhanging pines broke the wind and caught many of the flakes before they reached the ground.

Soon, the road-weary travelers huddled around a crackling fire, seeking whatever warmth they could soak from the flames and the growing mound of embers. Holt and Gallarath pulled a few heavy logs close to the blaze, so at least they had places to sit.

"There's a dry spot under here," the Daryman told Danis, pointing to a smooth patch of ground cushioned by pine needles, under the low branches of a towering fir. "Why don't you spread your bedroll here? The rest of us can find places over there." He gestured to the far side of the fire, allowing his eyes to flick across the prince, the knight, and the earl. Gallarath and Erik nodded and shrugged, while Terrence—his teeth chattering despite the fire—looked longingly at the relatively snug shelter.

"I'm ready to turn in," the princess announced, standing up and stretching. She threw her bedroll under the tree and then went to tend Lancer—the six horses were sheltered in a nearby hollow, well protected from the wind. Sir Ira, who had rejoined them late in the day, had declared that he would sleep there and keep an eye on the animals.

The men sat in silence, staring at the flames, each wrapped in his own thoughts. The only sound —except for the wind—was the clicking of the earl's teeth, though that noise subsided as the fire drove some of the chill from his bones. Danis was gone for several minutes, but none of the suitors left the fire to seek her.

Knowing that the lords would quickly intervene if they suspected that he had gone to speak to her, Holt rose and mumbled something about getting more firewood. He trudged into the woods opposite the direction of the horses, then circled the camp beyond sight and hearing of the other men. The snow was not yet deep, but it muffled the sounds of his movement enough to allow the Daryman to hasten after the princess.

He walked as much by feel as by sight—beyond the fire the night was almost totally black. He barely saw snowflakes inches from his eyes, and anything farther away vanished in the darkness. Still, he had cleared a good path over the short distance to the horses' shelter, and he had no difficulty finding the spot.

Something glimmered through the snow—a soft illumination like a halo around a dark shape. Stepping closer he realized that he was looking at the princess's back, and she was apparently holding some bright object in her hands.

With a gasp of dismay, Holt realized what that object must be.

"Who's there?" snapped Danis, whirling and standing to confront the Daryman. Even in her haste she had stuffed the luminescent thing into her saddlebag. Holt could see a trickle of light spilling from beneath the flap. "What do you want?" she demanded when she recognized him.

Douglas Niles

"You brought it, didn't you?" he retorted, whispering angrily. "You brought the Crown of Vanderthan!"

"I—well, it's mine!" she replied, dropping her voice to his quiet pitch.

He groaned softly. "It's the most powerful, the most dangerous artifact in all Karawenn! You were going to keep it locked up, safe—from *everyone!*"

"I didn't put it on! If I had, I probably would have known you were spying on me!"

"I wasn't *spying!* I was worried—"

"You sneaked up on me in the dark and watched what I was doing! I'd call *that* spying!" she spat back, taking the offensive. "And besides, I just brought it because—well, because I thought that this is where I might *need* it. I mean, maybe the thing that prophecy warned me about—maybe that's why I got the crown in the first place! So I'd be ready to face this threat that could destroy my entire family!"

The Daryman shook his head in frustration. Both he and Danis had experienced the unique power of the crown—the wearer could sense hidden dangers, could compel others to obey his will simply by voicing a command. At the same time, that person experienced a cold, aloof state that transcended friendship, love, or affection—such concerns became less than trivial.

In their cases, both the princess and the Daryman had—through an effort of will—removed the crown. At the same time, they had recognized the threat posed by the artifact, should it fall into the wrong hands.

"Besides," Danis added bitterly, "if there ever was a time when I was surrounded by brave protectors, this would seem to be it!"

Stung, Holt turned away, and as he did the wind carried a tiny suggestion of sodden wool to his nostrils. Surprised, he remembered that the fire—and hence the suitors—were *downwind* from here. He could not have smelled anything from the camp.

"What is it?" Danis demanded as he pushed his way through the underbrush to a nearby tree. Even in the darkness of the storm, muddy impressions were visible behind it—footprints! Several had already filled with snow, while the others obscured before his eyes.

"You haven't been over to this tree, have you?" he asked the princess. She shook her head, immediately understanding his meaning.

"Someone *else* was spying," he said. The tracks started in the direction of the camp, but when he tried to follow he lost them at the first place where the wind blew freely across the path.

"Do you think they saw?" the princess wondered, her voice hushed with fear.

"We can't know," Holt said miserably. "But don't let the crown out of your sight!"

"It's buried in the bottom of my saddlebag, under my spare cloak," she replied. "I guess I could put it in my bedroll whenever we camp."

"Do that," Holt said, his tone angrier than he wanted it to be. In truth, he could understand her fears—the smoky apparition in the throne room had been terrifying—and sympathize with her desire to use every advantage she could gain. He wondered if he was as frightened of the crown on *her* head as on some usurper's. The memory of her aloof, uncaring expression as she had worn it returned to him now, adding to his chill.

These thoughts dragged him down as he checked Old Thunder, collected some dry sticks and, with Danis, plodded back to the fire. Holt was pleased to see that the suitors had already retired, sparing him the need to explain his long firewood search.

Snug in his oiled deerskin bedroll, with the lush fur warm against his skin, Holt had no difficulty sleeping—indeed, he welcomed the snow as a pleasant alternative to rain. Fenrald, Danis, and Sir Erik also coped well with the cold weather, and with the chill dawn Prince Gallarath made a brave show of shaking out his sodden cloak and sticking his feet into slush-encrusted boots.

The mound that was Earl Terrence sneezed, sending a cloud of snow showering off his shivering form. The noble all but whimpered as they saddled their horses and embarked on the road.

This far up the valley the road was actually more of a trail, wide enough in places only for a single rider, and never for more than two abreast.

The snow continued to fall in big, wet flakes, and the horses clopped on messy ground, often slipping on mud-covered rocks.

Around them the blanket of forest gradually gave way to rising shoulders of moss-covered bluff, and finally into sheer and craggy cliffs. The heights vanished into the blustery sky, giving Holt the feeling that they traveled like mice through a vast, giant's hallway. The ceiling overhead was a murky mass of gloomy cloud, showering a steadily increasing volume of snow.

They reached a small inn just before dark, where a solid bridge crossed the much-narrowed Tannyv. The travelers found welcome shelter beside a cheery fire, and enjoyed the snug warmth of tiny but clean rooms. The Forest Heights Lodge, according to the innkeeper, was the last lowland inn; tomorrow, he told them, they would cross the great river and begin the climb toward the mountains.

"Another day or two and I'll be turning toward Graywall," Fenrald told Holt as they retired to the room they would share. "I could go from here, but I guess it won't hurt to see you through the first of the Trollheights."

"Thanks," Holt replied, forlorn at the prospect of his friend's departure.

It came as no surprise to Holt when, in the morning, Earl Terrence refused to continue on the quest. The suitor announced through sniffles and sneezes that as soon as the weather cleared he would embark for his realm of Amana—having more important things to attend to than the recovery of some legendary farm animal! The others bid him farewell. Erik and Gallarath, with condescending smiles, expressed much concern over Terrence's health.

The snow had ceased overnight, and the companions crossed the bridge, then forged along a trail barely discernable beneath a six-inch blanket of white. They were in the mountains now, with great foothills rising to both sides, and the winding canyon floor climbing steadily as they worked toward the higher peaks. The trail no longer bore any resemblance to a road—it became a footpath, winding, steep, and treacherous.

Sometime in the late afternoon it began to snow again. This time, thick, white flakes came down hard—and showed no sign of letting up.

10
Trollheights

"Ah—smell that fresh air!"

Prince Gallarath's suggestion awakened Holt from the snug confines of his fur-lined bedroll. The Daryman pulled back the flap that sheltered his face and inhaled a deep lungful—of pure frost.

The scion of Rochester was already moving about the camp, clapping his hands together before he dusted a thick layer of snow off his saddle and gear. Groaning, Holt emerged from his own cocoon, hurriedly throwing on a cloak and forcing his feet into snow-caked boots. With similar protestations, Danis and Sir Erik emerged into a crisp winter morning.

A small bundle of snow on the branch of a nearby tree suddenly shuddered, sloughing to the ground in a glistening cascade. Sir Ira, revealed, sniffed and stretched, shaking his wings to remove the powdery remnants of his blanket. "I say," he murmured, blinking against the sunlit view, "morning comes early in the mountains, doesn't it?"

Like the prince, Fenrald had risen early, apparently unfazed by the stinging chill. Now the dwarf clumped back to the camp, a great load of dried pine boughs in his arms. Within a few minutes he had a crackling fire blazing, and as Holt stomped his feet and felt circulation return to his numbed limbs, he finally began to feel somewhat awake.

For the first time, the Daryman noticed that the heavy clouds of the past few days had blown away. The sky overhead was a pure blue, diluted slightly with a winter pallor fading almost to white along the horizon.

And what a horizon! Though Holt had known by the rugged trail that they had entered the Trollheight Mountains, the glowering weather had prevented any real view of their surroundings. Now he saw a pair of high, snow-swept ridges flanking their deep valley. Sheer faces of icicle-draped rock crested one of the heights, while the other rose more gradually through a forest of dark, fragrant pine.

As he looked forward, the Daryman saw the

ridges open into a vista of high mountains. At least half a dozen peaks soared upward within the narrow gap of his view, jutting like ice-covered cones into the frosty sky. Slopes of dark rock, crowned by sweeping cornices of pure white snow, made these summits both beautiful and forbidding. For several minutes Holt stared in silent awe, stirred by nature's majesty.

Behind and below them the valley curled away, the curving ridges quickly blocking any view of the lowlands. The Daryman found it hard to believe that the River Tannyv and the rolling woodlands of Vanderthan lay close beyond the rugged heights.

"Some sight, eh?" Fenrald said, joining Holt as the Daryman stepped to the crest of a low promontory beside their camp.

"They look like the true masters of the world," the Daryman said quietly. "Remote and aloof— soaring above our petty concerns."

"And utterly unaffected by them," Danis noted as she too paused to admire the view.

"Everybody warmed up?" inquired Prince Gallarath, throwing the blanket and saddle over his stolid charger. "We'd best be starting on the trail."

Sighing, Holt and the others prepared their own horses. Old Thunder snorted a cloud of steam as the Daryman urged him from the sheltered bower of several close-set pines. Throwing clumps of snow over the coals of their fire, the companions once again took to the trail.

Sir Ira, declaring that he wanted to do some looking around, disappeared into a high valley—after promising to rejoin the companions in the future.

On the ground the snow was several feet deep, but this was only a drawback for Fenrald's short-legged pony. The others took turns leading the way, breaking a wide trough through the glittering, powdery crystals.

Before them the rising valley split into several different passages. One of these curved toward the right, descending into a lower gorge along a sweeping cliff of sheer, gray stone. Two other vales rose and vanished into the tumultuous chaos of peaks.

"Yonder lies Graywall," Fenrald announced, pointing into the descending vale. "Wherever that goat is, you'll find it in the highlands—to the left, there, I'd wager. So I guess our ways will be parting soon."

"Can you make it through the snow?" asked the Daryman.

"No problem—it's downhill, and once I get into the lee of the wall there'll be very little of it on the ground."

"How do you know that?" To Holt, the terrain leading toward Graywall looked very similar to the rest of the mountain range.

"Experience," Fenrald declared. "That's why we built it there—shelter from the storm, and easily defended against trolls."

Suitors Duel

"Are there trolls around here?" asked Holt, masking his concern with a light tone. He remembered with a shiver of horror his father's tale of Oxvale's destruction.

"Not this low," Fenrald said with a wave of his hand. "For a hundred years they haven't dared to venture out of the far wilderness—except for a few bands during the Troll War. None of them survived, I can attest."

"Too bad," Prince Gallarath muttered in apparent sincerity. "I have not yet had the chance to wet my axe blade with the blood of a troll."

"Be careful of your regrets," Fenrald attested. "It's not enough to just, as you say, 'wet your blade' when you're fighting trolls. You've got to burn them up, or whatever wounds you inflict will heal—practically as fast as you can cut another one!"

"*I'm* in no hurry to find them," Danis agreed. "It's to the wine-goat and back home, as far as I'm concerned."

"Good thinking. And you stay alert—keep these men in line, too," Fenrald said with gruffness that could not mask his deep affection.

The dwarf shook hands with Holt. "Remember, you're welcome in Graywall when this is over—and that's not just an option. If you don't give me the chance to pay you back for a summer of hospitality, I'll be comin' to get you! You can count on that!"

"I'll be there," Holt said with a laugh. His heartiness didn't conceal his own sadness, and he realized that he'd truly miss one of the greatest friends he'd ever known.

Fenrald started across the valley. True to his prediction, the dwarf's little pony forged easily through the soft snow, following the generally descending line of a shallow creek—though now the stream, as well as the surrounding boulders, were fully buried beneath the wintery blanket.

As the dwarf, cloaked in a huge fur, dwindled into the distance, the Daryman felt a pang of loneliness. Of course, he would return to Vanderthan with Danis—he owed her that much—but before it came time for the king to announce the winner of the contest, Holt thought he would try to get some little distance away from the city. Graywall seemed like a good destination.

Overhead Sir Ira banked and soared, cutting back and forth across their path, apparently unaffected by the chilly air. By mutual consent the companions started toward the nearest of the side valleys. They climbed a long, gradual slope that tired the horses with its vast size more than its steepness.

Realizing that the horses were too heavily laden to make the ascent, the humans dismounted, taking turns plowing through the soft barrier. Though the air was ice-cold, the winds remained calm and the sky clear, so that after an hour Holt threw open his cloak and cast back his hood. He realized with surprise that he was soaked with sweat.

Danis was uncharacteristically quiet. Holt wondered if she, too, missed the hearty companionship of their dwarven friend. Prince Gallarath and Sir Erik were no substitute for the loyal Fenrald.

Finally they crested the upward slope, entering another low valley flanked by a pair of jagged, rock-faced heights. There was only one way to go—along the valley floor—so without discussion Sir Erik, who was in the lead, started along the level ground.

"Ah—this is the stuff of adventure!" Prince Gallarath proclaimed, thumping his chest and drawing a deep lungful of air. "The peaks—the sky! The view!"

Wincing under the onslaught of enthusiasm, Holt turned away. He looked past Sir Erik, noting an odd assortment of snowdrifts that mounded upward very near their intended path. These small hummocks of snow were scattered over a wide area of the valley floor. Why would the wind create such small drifts, he wondered—indeed, *how* could it happen?

One of the mounds suddenly shivered, snow exploding outward in a violent shower. Holt gaped at a horrific image within that snowy explosion—a fang-filled mouth and two hands studded with long, curved talons. Above the widespread maw the Daryman beheld an even more awful sight:

two eyes of utter, lightless black, yawning like twin pits in the grotesque and monstrous face.

They were hopeless, lifeless holes, and Holt instinctively understood why: they were eyes of Entropy, glowering in the face of a servant of that dark sphere. A troll!

Sir Erik's horse whinnied in panic as the knight quickly drew his gleaming sword. At the same time, the other mounds of snow shivered and dissolved, each revealing an evil creature concealed within.

The trolls were surprisingly huge, rising well over the height of a man. Their bodies were thin, but taut with wiry sinew, and they uttered gurgling growls of inhuman savagery. The beasts advanced at shocking speed toward the companions.

Dissuaded by Sir Erik's gleaming sword, the first of the brutes dodged around the knight and leaped straight at Holt. Swinging the Lodestone Blade instinctively—he didn't even remember drawing the weapon—Holt chopped savagely, cutting the beast down. It twitched in the soft snow, and he stabbed it again to still its struggles.

Prince Gallarath, mounted upon his snorting charger, rode past Holt, slashing with his axe against a pair of trolls. The creatures fell, driven down by the blows of the weapon and the force of the huge horse, but as soon as the nobleman passed, the trolls sprang back to their feet. Holt stared in horror as he saw the deep cut in the face of a wounded monster mend itself.

Shaking off his shock, the Daryman lunged forward, cutting down first one, then the other of the two brutes with the Lodestone Blade. He saw that the sword of gray, true to its ancient enchantment, left wounds that did not heal in the bodies of the grotesque predators.

Danis screamed and Holt whirled to see a troll dragging her away from the kicking Lancer. Sir Ira dived at the beast's head, but the troll knocked the courageous owl away with a swipe of its claws.

Desperately Holt lunged, driving the tip of his blade into the monster, bringing the beast hissing and spitting around to face him. The huge, taloned forepaw knocked him backward, and as he went down he saw the creature reaching toward his unprotected belly.

Abruptly the beast screamed, the sound a shrill, piercing shriek. Recovering from her terror, Danis had stabbed it in the back. Though the wound would heal, she caused the creature great pain. When it whirled to face her, Holt scrambled forward and slew it.

Old Thunder reared and snorted in the midst of a circle of trolls, and the Daryman hacked his way through the ring, mounting the pitching steed with difficulty. Danis and the two nobles were already astride their horses, while Sir Ira soared away, struggling to gain altitude.

"Ride!" cried Prince Gallarath. "Ride for your lives!" Behind him, several trolls climbed back to their feet, emerging from pits of black snow where they had shed their inky blood.

Holt gagged in horror as he saw a severed arm crawl toward the lurching troll that had lost it. With its good hand the beast planted the arm against the wound—and it held!

Sir Erik's charger knocked several trolls out of the way, and frantically the knight gestured to Danis. The princess galloped after him while Gallarath and Holt hacked at the pursuing trolls, driving them back for a moment, giving the two men time to race after their companions.

Fortunately a low rise of stony ground meandered along the valley floor, and the wind had blown most of the snow free from this snakelike moraine. The horses pounded along the smooth ground through only a few inches of powder, quickly leaving the gangly, loping trolls behind.

Still, the monsters followed tenaciously. The wiry beasts jogged in the tracks of the horses, several dozen of the brutes stretching into a long, deadly column. Occasionally they barked, snarled, or howled, but for the most part they ran with silent and deadly determination.

Gradually the valley floor circled upward, sweeping between dense forests of snow-covered pines. In a few places the rocky moraine was interrupted and the horses were forced to flounder through

deep snow. Each time they found more solid ground, however, maintaining their lead—though Holt was dismayed to see that they couldn't seem to pull away from their grotesque pursuers.

Laboring up another steep slope, the companions entered a high, narrow valley. Here there were no trees. Instead, glimmering columns of ice—waterfalls that had frozen in full flow—dangled from the high cliffs around this vale. Yet as they raced forward, Holt felt a growing sense of despair—they had ridden into a box canyon, with no apparent means of escape.

But when he looked back he observed a curious and hopeful sign. The trolls, who showed no sign of fatigue, halted at the mouth of this valley. They watched the companions with those horrific, deadly eyes, yet they made no move to advance.

It seemed that, for the moment at least, the company was safe.

11
Winterbeard

Moving farther into the high valley, the companions followed the curve of the ground, gradually coming around a shoulder of mountain that had screened their full view. As they rode the trudging horses, their eyes frequently scanned the rear horizon, seeking any sign of pursuit.

They approached a steep, angled wall of rock that sloped into the valley from one of the ridges. Veering to the side, they sought to go around the obstacle.

"What's that?" asked Holt, as a glimmering cone of white ice caught his eye, jutting above the edge of rock that sheared across their path. Another, similar shape came into view, and when they advanced a little more they moved past the rocky barrier and stopped, staring upward in awe.

The white spires Holt had seen each capped a similarly alabaster column. A dozen of these towers jutted upward from a wall of slick, gleaming ice—and that wall encircled a towering palace. The structure was nearly as large as Castle Vanderthan, and was apparently made entirely of ice.

Although they still couldn't see the base of that great, circular wall, they were close enough to observe tiny windows carved in the walls of the towers. The palace keep was a multitiered structure, rising to a great central tower. No pennants flew from the heights, nor was there any other sign to indicate that the place was inhabited. Still, the Daryman felt beyond any doubt that their approach was being observed.

"The trolls! That's why they stopped—because they fear this place!" Danis exclaimed in sudden understanding. "But . . . *why* do they fear it?"

"An enemy of the brutes could prove to be a friend of ours," Prince Gallarath observed. "Perhaps the lady would care to wait here while I ride ahead to investigate?"

"Thanks—but we'll go together," Danis replied.

The castle was still, apparently abandoned. No tracks marred the wide sweep of snow around the mighty structure, although a 'gate'—really a sheet of bluish ice where the doorway should be—blocked access.

Abruptly the Daryman sensed movement around them, and as he whirled in his saddle he saw numerous hulking shapes emerge from the snow. Rising onto their rear legs, the shaggy beings took a few steps forward and held the party of companions completely surrounded.

"The same trick as the trolls!" sputtered the prince in dismay.

"Only these fellows did it better," Holt noted. Until the beasts stood, the Daryman had noticed absolutely no irregularity in the smooth surface of the snow cover.

"Smugglers!" boomed a great voice, and the largest of the shaggy snowmen advanced belligerently to confront them.

"Not smugglers, but pilgrims," Danis said, quickly urging Lancer forward to face the creature. To Holt's surprise, both the prince and the knight let her pass. "We come seeking shelter—and ask you, honored lord, if you will grant our request."

"Treachery!" shouted the beast, with enough force to rock Danis back in her saddle. "You come with soft words—but such words can conceal the icy sword of deceit!"

"Such words can also be nothing more than the truth!" the princess snapped. "Who are you to accuse us?"

Douglas Niles

"I am Winterbeard, warchief of the Free Yetis!" claimed the creature, spreading his arms wide as if to display his full magnificence.

Holt admitted, grudgingly, that the beast was not perhaps so grotesque as he had first perceived. Though Winterbeard's face and body were covered in shaggy, white fur, his low-hanging brows revealed eyes of startling blue. His visage was undeniably fierce, yet he moved his lips and tongue as smoothly as any man.

The yeti towered over the humans, and if he wasn't quite as tall as a troll, Winterbeard nevertheless outweighed those horrid monsters by a good measure. Where trolls were gangly and lean, the yeti possessed broad shoulders, barrel chests, and long, very muscular arms. Their legs were short, almost dwarflike, but the yeti seemed to move even through deep snow with little difficulty.

"Why do you call us smugglers?" demanded Danis after she haughtily studied the creature for a few heartbeats.

"You approach the castle of my dire foe, Frostcrown—and I believe you seek entrance there!" declared Winterbeard, dropping his fists to his hips and glaring at the party of humans.

"I assure you that, until a moment ago, we knew of neither yourself nor your dire enemy. Is Frostcrown, perhaps, a troll?" wondered Danis.

"Insults!" roared Winterbeard, all but spitting in his outrage. "He may be a low, vile, despicable creature—but dare not compare him to an evil troll!"

"Is he a man?"

"Nay! He be a yeti, like myself—but unworthy of the true Ice Mantle! We give him the title chief of the Slave Yetis! For years he be hiding in this palace, and we not let him out. Nor do we let anyone go in, to take him food and stuff. Those who try get chopped as smugglers."

"Er, *chopped?*" inquired Prince Gallarath, urging his charger to Lancer's side. "Surely it's not necessary to take extreme—"

"Silence!" boomed Winterbeard, and the prince quickly obeyed.

Holt, meanwhile, looked around them, trying to assess their prospects for escape. He was forced to admit that they were bleak. The four riders were at the center of some three dozen yetis. The creatures stood almost arm to arm in an encircling ring. Briefly the Daryman looked upward, wondering where Sir Ira was. He saw no sign of the owl, but the fact did not surprise him. Wise and powerful though he was, Sir Ira could do very little to help them here.

"What is your devious aim, Winterbeard?" Another voice joined the fray, this one booming from the ramparts of the Ice Castle.

"Ha, Frostcrown! I have taken your smugglers in a neat trap! Do you care to watch their disposal?"

"Not *my* smugglers," retorted the voice atop the wall. Holt saw a hulking yeti there, leering toward them with his face locked in a fierce snarl. "D'you seek to deceive me with false news?"

"Cease your lies!" cried Winterbeard. "Or I shall vent my displeasure upon your human lackeys!"

Fervently hoping Frostcrown could hold his tongue, the Daryman looked back to the ramparts. He was puzzled, and not terribly relieved, to see that the looming chieftain had disappeared.

Abruptly the gate of the castle—a smooth portal of hazy blue ice—toppled outward, releasing a cascade of tiny frost chips as it broke away from the wall. Booming onto the ground, the opening revealed Frostcrown glowering furiously at Winterbeard.

Marching deliberately over the gate, the yeti newcomer stomped up to the opposing chieftain, blue eyes flashing with deep fury.

"You may insult my heritage . . . mock my honesty . . . taunt my progeny . . . but—and hear this well, Wint—do not *ever* accuse me of resorting to human lackeys! Do you understand?"

"My apologies," Winterbeard declared, surprising Holt with his humble tone. "I'm afraid I got carried away in the fervor of the moment. Of course, I should have known that, loathsome and craven though you be, such would not be the case."

"Right you are," Frostcrown warned, slightly mollified.

"Would you care to join in the executions?" Winterbeard asked politely.

Danis stared in shock while Holt shook his head, unwilling to believe what he heard. A part of him wanted to laugh at the bizarre misunderstandings of the snow-creatures, but the seriousness of their situation was all too plain.

"What kind of a war is this?" the Daryman demanded in exasperation. He pointed to the open gate of the castle. A few yetis lolled around there, but they could have been quickly overcome if Winterbeard had ordered a sudden rush. He didn't favor either of the yetis—both, in fact, were kind of frightening—but he couldn't understand their ignoring of the battle in favor of this ludicrous debate.

"Careful, smuggler—do not insult us!" warned Frostcrown.

"We're *not* smugglers!" Danis retorted angrily. "You should know that! After all, he thinks we're working for you!"

"Don't try any tricks of logic!" bellowed the yeti, shaking his shaggy head.

"Do you think we're smuggling food?" asked Holt, biting back his own frustration to keep his voice level.

"You bet!"

"Well, where's all this food, then?" The Daryman gestured to the four lightly-laden horses. "We don't have enough to feed one of you for more than a few days!"

The yetis scowled, apparently stumped by the question.

"Why are you fighting each other, anyway?" Danis asked quietly.

"We want to get the castle—it's our turn, but Frostcrown and his Slave Yetis are keeping us out," Winterbeard said bluntly. "It's his accursed stubbornness and selfishness that's to blame!"

"The castle is ours!" declared Frostcrown, crossing his arms firmly.

"It looks pretty big to me," Prince Gallarath observed helpfully. "I'm sure if—"

"It's not as big as it looks!" snapped the chief of the Slave Yetis. "Only one good cave, down low."

"Couldn't you use more of it?" Holt wondered. "I mean, there's got to be *lots* of space in there." He gestured to the sweeping walls, rising high above them.

"We can't share it. We're two different clans— And I'm not going in there with this sneaky little lowland snow weasel!" snarled the latter chieftain.

"And I'm not letting you into the castle, you ugly, mangy, flea-bitten son of a mountain goat!" replied Frostcrown.

"Are you ready to resume the war?" Winterbeard demanded.

"It will take a little time to get the gate fixed— but then, yes, of course I am!"

"Um, I know this is a matter for wise warchiefs. As a humble human, I don't dare give you suggestions," Holt said, choosing his words carefully. "But what if one of you was to have an idea—perhaps a way that two clans can become one. You could all live there, then. Of course, I don't know if that's the kind of idea a yeti could—"

"What are you implying, human?" growled Frostcrown, his voice rumbling with menace.

"Do you call us stupid?" Winterbeard chimed in.

"Never!" the Daryman protested, raising both his hands. "Surely one of you will have that idea—very soon!"

"You bet we will!" Apparently soothed, Winterbeard turned back to his fellow chieftain. "Now, about the war—"

"Say—I'm having an idea," Frostcrown interrupted. He studied the sheer wall of the fortress, shaking his head. "What if our two clans could, somehow, become one?"

"And how to do that?"

"I know a way," Danis said. "Where I come from, there are wise leaders—diplomats. They meet together, and make agreements called 'treaties.' With a treaty, you could agree to make your two tribes into one!"

"And we would live inside the big cave?" Winterbeard inquired.

"Of course—there's plenty of room. No reason to make you sleep outside in the snow, when you could come in and have a bed of solid ice!"

"Splendid!" The two chieftains clasped hands and turned triumphantly to the humans.

"Um, do you suppose we might be going?" asked Danis hesitantly, looking toward the heights of the valley.

"Going? That could be dangerous—there's *trolls* out there! Give 'em a day to cool heels—they don't have smart rememberies like yetis. By tomorrow they'll forget why they're there."

"Trolls?" Prince Gallarath scoffed. "Why, we hacked our way through a legion of the brutes. Don't think that they hold any fear for us!"

"Just the same," Danis said, "it would be better if we *didn't* have to fight every step of the way. Perhaps we should wait, as this wise chieftain has suggested."

"Splendid!" boomed both yetis together. Frost-crown swept his hand expansively toward the looming gate of the castle. "Come in, then—all of you! While we wait for the trolls to forget, you shall all enjoy the splendors of a victory feast!"

Holt thought it impolitic to point out that neither force had actually won the war. Instead, he sighed in relief, then smiled broadly as he saw Danis grin and flash him a wink. Soon the ice blue walls of the castle closed around them.

12
Icekeep

Everywhere around the feast hall, yetis pushed
and jostled, barking and growling at each other.
The air was filled with a chorus of snarling oaths
and belligerent challenges. Cuffs and blows sent
many of the hulking humanoids stumbling about
the huge chamber, and these tumbles inevitably
led to further collisions, arguments, and punches.

And the party was just beginning, Holt realized.

He and Sir Erik followed the prince and princess through the throng. Winterbeard and Frostcrown, arm in arm, swaggered among the mass of
their clans, striding toward a raised platform of ice

that occupied the center of the room. The chief of the Free Yetis had just showed the companions a spacious chamber where he said they could sleep in comfort. The icy walls and benches were lined with furs, and the Daryman had been inclined to believe him. But there would be no rest, the creatures insisted, until after the feast.

"A thought," Erik said quietly, speaking to the Daryman out of the corner of his mouth. "We'd be advised to keep our purpose in the Trollheights a secret. For all we know, these brutes have some sort of feeling for the Black Goat. It's not likely that they'd take kindly to our attempt at capture."

"Good point," Holt agreed. There were probably very few treasured objects or creatures in these barren heights—it seemed easily conceivable that the yetis, if they knew about the goat, would hold the creature in some kind of esteem.

"Let's tell the others," the Grand Knight of Rockeford suggested.

Jostling forward, Holt reached the First Daughter's side and made the suggestion to her. She readily agreed, while beside her Prince Gallarath nodded thoughtfully to Sir Erik.

"So—join us for the feast!" boomed Winterbeard, gesturing to the four humans to climb onto the platform with the two chieftains.

"It will be good that you can tell your peoples of the wisdom and tolerance of the yeti," Frostcrown added.

Abruptly, the creature's shaggy brow furrowed in deep thought. "You say that you are not smugglers, and we believe you. But pray, what is the purpose that brings you so far above the human realms?"

"We are explorers," Sir Erik said smoothly. "We seek a pass through the mountains to see if we can open travel to the realms beyond."

"A worthy goal," Frostcrown conceded. "But doomed to failure. It is known to us that the Trollheights climb higher and higher, until they blend with the sky itself. There is no crossing—no other side."

"Like World's End," Holt mused. "Another border of Karawenn."

"And, like the sea that flows into Thunder Deep, a barrier to landbound man," Danis agreed with a sigh. For a moment her green eyes sparked, and she looked as though she wanted to cross those unscalable heights, to lay her eyes on the unknown lands beyond.

"By the Black Goat—enough of this prattling!" Winterbeard exclaimed. "Bring forth the wine!" At the words Holt and Danis locked eyes, then quickly looked apart.

Several young yetis, bearing heavy sheepskins that had been sewn into great winesacks, passed through the crowd, offering rich, red drink to the assembled yetis. One came up and quenched the thirst of the chieftains, and then offered wine to

the four humans. They each took a taste of the
stuff, and Holt privately decided that it was in fact
the finest wine he had ever tasted—dry and smooth,
with a hint of distinctive musk. Yet the companions declined further drinks, watching as the
potent stuff overcame the reserves of the rambunc-
tious snowmen.

"How do you make such splendid wine?" asked
Danis, casually dropping the question as Winterbeard lowered the skin for the fifth time.

The chieftain's whiskers dripped with wine, and
he smacked his lips in pleasure before he replied.
"It is a thing known only to us—a magical secret.
It is splendid, is it not? Come, share our drink with
us. Soon we will feast."

Danis feigned another drink, agreeing with the
yeti's assessment.

Shortly other young snowmen brought great
platters and bowls made from ice, filled with a
variety of foodstuffs. Holt and the others sampled
chilled fish, an icy salad of lichen and moss, as well
as a variety of frosty concoctions favored with vari-
ous types of fruits and sugars. Though there was
not a warm element to the meal, the Daryman
found it filling and invigorating—not to mention
quite tasty.

Throughout it all, the two chieftains kept up a
lively debate, spiced by an occasional bellowed
command for more food or drink. Several other
times the oath—'by the Black Goat'—was repeated

by each, and the companions could not help looking at each other in acknowledgment.

"Magical wine?" Danis asked once again, as the skins made their increasingly messy rounds. "I would think that even magical grapes would have a hard time growing in this climate."

"Hah!" crowed Winterbeard. "That's the secret—the magic is so potent that no grapes are needed! We simply make the ascent to the Three Hags, and—"

"The Free Yetis always talk too much!" snapped Frostcrown testily.

Winterbeard's mouth clapped shut abruptly, and he scowled at the companions suspiciously, apparently trying to decide if he'd been indiscreet. He scratched his sloping forehead, not at all certain of what, exactly, he'd revealed.

"This is a splendid castle," Holt remarked quickly. "There seems to be lots of room for all of you. Is it very old?"

"Been here forever," Frostcrown breezily asserted.

"Yup. Ten years and hundred times or somethin'—since the Warm Years ended," Winterbeard added.

"Do you know who built it?" Holt asked.

"Some guys," the two chieftains replied, with a mutual shrug indicating that, to them, one guy was pretty much like another.

"Best caves here, of anywhere!" Frostcrown declared. "We like 'em plenty." He turned to his counterpart. "Good thing for you we let you in. As a matter of fact—"

"As a matter of fact, *what?*" growled Winterbeard, glowering at the other chief. Gazes locked, the two yetis bristled furiously, baring fangs and raising the rough white fur on their hackles.

"Perhaps we should retire to our quarters," Holt suggested very quietly to Danis while the two yetis focused on their steadily growing quarrel.

"Good idea. I think we can make our apologies in the morning," the princess conceded.

Indeed, the frost chieftains had risen to their feet and now faced off belligerently. Discreetly the princess led her companions down from the platform, thankful that the snowmen's quarrel held the chieftain's attention. Though they had not yet come to blows, the tenor of the argument grew increasingly harsh.

"Should we get out of the castle altogether?" Prince Gallarath wondered as the humans made their way down the abandoned hallway leading to their quarters.

Holt reflected on the wilderness of ice and snow that lay beyond the walls. "I think we'll get a lot more rest—not to mention be more comfortable—if we stay here. Otherwise we'll have to sleep in a snowdrift, and without a fire, since there doesn't seem to be a tree for miles. Are you willing to risk the yetis changing their minds about their hospitality?" he asked Danis.

"Yes," she replied without hesitation. "Despite the bickering tonight, I think they've resolved the dispute that led to war. Besides, I suspect they'll be sleeping late in the morning."

The First Daughter's suspicions proved correct, as the faint light of dawn seeped through the bluish walls of the Ice Castle. Not a yeti stirred as Holt emerged from their room and looked both ways along the hall. Stealthily creeping toward the throne room, he was relieved to find their horses in the great, frost-walled chamber where they had left them, and absolutely delighted when he saw that the castle gate still lay open, where Frost-crown had knocked it over on the previous day.

Quickly the four humans mounted their steeds and rode through the gate, starting up the valley floor that exited the vale on the uphill side.

"I wonder about Sir Ira," Danis said as the Ice Castle receded behind them. "Of course, he's likely to go off by himself now and then, but I hope nothing's happened to him."

"That owl can take care of himself," Sir Erik assured her. "From what I've seen, he's worth a company of seasoned footmen—and a skilled captain."

"Sir Ira is a remarkable bird," Holt agreed.

"He's not really a bird, he told me," Danis noted. "He's actually a Hsiao." She spelled the word, which sounded like hss-SHOW when she spoke it. "When the elves fled the Knollbarrens, he and his kin took over many of the wild places, especially the most sacred groves and meadows."

"There are others like him?" Sir Erik asked curiously.

"He thinks there are, but he hasn't seen any since the Troll War," Danis explained.

The companions could deduce nothing further about Sir Ira's whereabouts, and soon their attention was consumed by the climb. Though the slope was steeper than others they had crossed, most of the snow had tumbled away, and the horses had little difficulty with the grade. As an added bonus, the sky remained clear, soaring overhead in its pale, wintry blue.

Before noon they crested the ridge, seeing another stretch of valleys spreading into several different directions. The snow lay deeper in the lower reaches, and vast drifts swept downward from the heights, forming formidable barriers to travel.

"Which way?" asked Danis, trying hard to bite back her despair.

"The yeti mentioned something about Three Hags," Sir Erik remembered.

Prince Gallarath indicated a trio of steep summits looming beyond the next valley. "What about those?" the nobleman wondered, pointing.

With a little imagination, Holt found that he could picture the face of an old woman in the foremost of the mountains. The pair beyond mimicked the shape of their sister closely enough that he could extend the illusion to create in his mind the image of three withered old crones.

"The Three Hags!" the Daryman declared. "They can be no others!"

"I agree," Sir Erik chimed in. "It looks as though there's a valley leading up to them—right there." The knight indicated a steep and snowy ravine that swept downward from the vicinity of the triple summits.

"We might do well to climb this more gentle slope," Holt suggested, pointing to the side.

"Nonsense!" interjected the prince of Rochester. "The most direct route is the best, I say."

"I agree," Sir Erik said firmly.

Danis looked at Holt and shrugged. "Let's climb the straight path. We might as well get it over with," she said.

As her green eyes turned upward, the Daryman saw a flash of apprehension, and wondered if the princess considered halting here and letting the men go on. He remembered vividly the dire prophecy that had spumed upward from the mirror in the throne room, and privately suspected that leaving her here might not be a bad idea. Still, he knew her far too well to suggest such a course of action—he would only be ridiculed for his caution. At the same time a very quiet inner voice whispered to him that she might need him, very badly. He would not risk her wrath on an argument he knew he would lose.

The stolid horses started up the incline, often lurching and skipping ahead in an effort to hold their momentum. After a few minutes of this, Holt dismounted, and without comment the others quickly followed suit. The underlying surface was solid rock, but the few inches of snow that had accumulated here made for treacherous footholds. Frequently one of the companions slid backward, landing face first on the hard ground, only to scramble upward and silently, determinedly, resume the ascent.

"You know, this goat seemed to be rather precious to the yetis," Prince Gallarath observed when they stopped to catch their breath. "I'll have to use care when I bring it down from the mountain. No use antagonizing the brutes, after all."

"*You* bring it down?" Sir Erik said with a snort of amusement. "It would seem that the matter of who captures the beast hasn't been decided yet."

"Quite so," the prince agreed cheerfully, giving the knight a good-natured smile. "I'll make my plans and talk about it later."

"We have other problems," Holt observed, looking at the sky. The others tilted their heads upward and saw that the stretch of clear weather quickly drew to a close. Dark gray clouds loomed over the high peaks, and as they watched, the billowing mass surged quickly closer. "Those are carrying snow—lots of it, unless I miss my guess."

"I'm afraid you're right," Danis groaned. "Where are we going to find shelter on this slope?"

"Nothing for it but to reach the top," the prince declared, still cheerful. "Perhaps we should pick up the pace a bit." Leading his weary charger, the Son of Rochester climbed past Holt, hurrying toward the summit of the pass. The Daryman took some satisfaction when, a few minutes later, he passed the prince—who had paused gasping for breath.

Gallarath quickly rejoined the procession, in the rear, while Holt and Sir Erik scrambled toward the relatively flat surface of a shelf on the wide mountainside.

"Look here!" cried the knight. Sir Erik approached a wide-mouthed cave that dipped into the wall at the back of the shelf. The shelter was not deep, but it was high and broad. Most importantly, the rocky ground within was free of snow.

"A place we can weather the storm," Holt agreed, eyeing the clouds that continued to darken the sky. As if to emphasize his words, snowflakes started to drift down, swirling past as the glowering overcast continued its inexorable march.

The four humans gathered in the crude shelter, leaving the horses to stand in the entrance. The big steeds, tails out, provided something like a fourth wall to the enclosure, and Holt decided that they might actually be secure here. Whether they would be able to continue after the snow passed—assuming it passed—was another question entirely, and one he was not prepared to consider.

"I think I saw a grove of trees off to the side," Sir Erik noted. "Perhaps I could get some wood—a fire, after all, could be a pleasant amenity."

"I didn't see any trees," Holt said. "Nothing but snow, ice, and rock."

"There weren't many," Erik explained. "But a few hardy cedars seemed to stick out through the snow."

"Do you think we can get there and back before the snow gets too heavy?" Prince Gallarath wondered. Even as he spoke, he rubbed his hands before him, as if soaking up the warmth of a crackling fire.

"I believe I can," the knight replied. "I think the rest of you should stay here, though. Blayze and I can bring enough wood back for an all-night fire—and there's no use risking more than one of us out there."

"I'll come with you," Holt offered. "We can bring wood for a few days—you never know if it might be necessary."

The knight smiled with a tolerant benevolence that inflamed the Daryman. At the same time, Gallarath's eyebrows shot upward in delight, and Holt realized that he'd offered to leave the princess alone with the prince in the shelter of their cave. He regretted his offer immediately, but he could not bring himself to retract his offer to help.

Fortunately, the knight himself came to Holt's

aid. "I'll bring plenty of wood," Sir Erik declared. "Why don't the rest of you just stay put?"

A pang of unease—probably guilt—tugged at Holt as their companion led his horse into the storm. They watched Sir Erik and Blayze vanish into the steadily growing storm, hoping devoutly that he would soon return with firewood.

An hour passed, then another. But it was not until full darkness settled around them that the companions acknowledged the likelihood: Sir Erik would not be coming back.

13
Search in the Snow

Night settled in with a vengeance, the darkening assault aided by heavy clouds and the increasingly thick flurries of large, wet snowflakes. The horses stomped their feet and shook their hindquarters, sending the snow cascading to the ground as the placid creatures prepared to weather the storm.

Within the cave, the mood was not so tranquil. Holt rose and paced, as much as the cramped shelter would allow. Gallarath sat and glowered, honing the blade of his battle-axe as his face reflected the variety of emotions, all unpleasant, that stormed through his mind.

"D'you think he went to find the goat himself?" the Son of Rochester finally asked, his voice a plaintive plea for reassurance.

Holt had considered the same possibility some hours earlier, and discarded it. "I don't think so. The weather's too bad to do much in the way of exploration, and we're a long way below those three peaks—even if they're the Three Hags the yetis talked about. No, I think he got lost on his search for wood. I hope he finds some way to get out of the storm."

"I think he will," Danis said. "Sir Erik seems well able to take care of himself."

Holt felt a flash of jealousy—he had noted no such competence in the knight! Danis's statement seemed to indicate that she had been paying considerable attention to Sir Erik. At the same time, he was slightly comforted by the fact that there was little warmth in her observance. His irritation was further quenched when he considered the miserable night that Sir Erik would no doubt spend—if he was still alive.

Without a fire, the three companions suffered terribly from the icy temperatures of the long, snowy night. They huddled together under every blanket and furskin they had, and though comfort was minimal, they all lived until the dawn. Holt slept for a few minutes at a time, until sharp edges of rock caused such pain that he was forced to shift his position for another brief respite.

Finally a dirty gray illumination penetrated the gloom beyond their cave. It was not sunrise by any stretch of the imagination, but Holt knew that daylight had again returned to Karawenn. The wind had died sometime after midnight, and though it had snowed for many more hours, the storm seemed to have lost its fury. Now, in the harsh light, the Daryman looked outward at a scene of placidly descending flakes.

"It's light," he told his companions as they stirred beneath the communal pile of blankets. "I'll go look for Erik." Only after he had spoken did he realize he had omitted the 'sir'. Such concerns, he told himself, meant less than nothing in the severe climate—their stakes were no less than survival itself.

"Shouldn't we stick together?" Danis asked, shivering as she emerged from the furry cover.

"We're already separated," Holt pointed out. "If I can find Erik and bring him back here, we'll be together again. If not, you . . . and the prince will still be able to continue with the quest. Besides, Old Thunder's the only horse with long enough legs to get through these drifts."

For a moment he thought she would argue with him, but at last the princess nodded reluctantly. She pulled the fur-lined bedroll close to her face. "Don't go too far—if you can't find any sign of him, come back here as soon as you can."

After promising to follow her suggestion, the Daryman saddled his stolid mount and started across the slope beyond their cave. The snow had fallen so thickly overnight that every trace of the knight's tracks was obliterated. Still, Holt remembered that Erik had pointed roughly in a southerly direction when he indicated the grove of trees, so the Daryman decided to follow along in that path.

Old Thunder plowed through a three-foot layer of powdery snow, raising each hoof in a cascade of crystals as he lumbered along. Hummocks and swales in the terrain caused the snow to collect in long drifts, but the big horse burst through these ridges—even those that rose to his neck.

At first Holt scanned the horizon before him for some sign of the small grove of trees—Sir Erik, after all, had started out for wood. Riding back and forth across the slope, however, Holt began to wonder if the knight had been imagining things.

In fact, the terrain became even more forbidding as the Daryman rode higher into the Trollheights. Narrow gorges, reminiscent of the ravines in the Knollbarrens, twisted away to each side. Forbidding walls of gray granite or rust-red ore formed a maze far more daunting than the hedges in the gardens of Castle Vanderthan.

Old Thunder came to a halt in the midst of a flat expanse that Holt suspected was probably a frozen lake. Examining the smooth surfaces of the surrounding slopes, the Daryman admitted to a feeling approaching despair. Wherever Sir Erik had gone, it seemed that his trail was long since buried in the storm.

A slight irregularity in the far ridgeline caught Holt's eye. He studied the place, and decided that he was looking at the trail of some large creature, such as a horse, that had worked its way through the snow.

It took him more than an hour to reach the place, but then his hunch was rewarded. He saw a niche between a pair of towering rocks where someone had taken shelter early in the storm. Holt felt certain that it had been Sir Erik. Though the tracks of arrival had disappeared, the departure trail was plainly carved through the smooth snow.

As he looked at the narrow shelter, the Daryman reflected that Sir Erik had probably been more snug than his three companions, who had not been effectively protected from the wind.

Warmed by a sense of relief—at least the knight was alive—Holt guided Old Thunder along the trail. Sir Erik had crossed the ridge and made his way through the steep, narrow valley beyond. Since the fresh-turned tracks of the snow were undisturbed, the Daryman knew that the suitor had not departed his shelter until after the snow had ceased. Still, he was probably several hours ahead.

Holt was surprised that the knight's trail continued away from the companions—apparently Sir Erik had been confused by the storm. He could wander these mountains for days without finding them, so the young farmer pressed Old Thunder ahead with growing urgency. At the same time, he began to wonder: was it in fact possible that the knight had left the companions to seek the goat on his own?

The narrow valley was not terribly deep, and since they had the advantage of following tracks that had already been pushed through the deep powder, the Daryman and his big horse made good time. At the next crest the path passed between a pair of towering knolls, each draped with gray cliffs and long tendrils of ice. The ground grew more rough, but Sir Erik had followed a winding gully that did not climb very steeply.

Holt wondered how the knight could have mistaken the direction since there had been no terrain anything like this on the initial portions of their ascent. It seemed more likely than ever that the knight had left them intentionally.

Abruptly the trail curved between two looming walls and then opened through a tight gap. Beyond, Holt saw a small, bowl-shaped valley surrounded by tall cliffs—indeed, this gorge seemed to be the only way to enter or leave, short of flying. A small stone hut stood near the base of the depression, and Sir Erik's horse was standing outside the little building. Steam rose from the creature's withers and snorted from its nostrils in the still, cold air.

Holt was about to shout a welcome when some vague reluctance held his tongue. He realized what it was: several other tracks led to the hut. They were narrower than the trough plowed by the knight's warhorse, but the Daryman could discern nothing else about them. Still, it seemed at least possible that Sir Erik was held captive by someone who would not welcome Holt's arrival. These tracks led to a small gap on the other side of the valley—a place Holt had not noticed before, but that seemed to offer an additional point of access to the place.

Abruptly a figure moved through the doorway, emerging into the sunlit bowl. The black armor, the shiny gloves were unmistakable—Holt recognized Sir Erik immediately. Still, the Daryman remained too cautious to shout. Instead, he waited and watched in the narrow cut in the rocks.

The Grand Knight of Rockeford held something white in his hand, which he raised toward the sky. A bird fluttered upward, released from the glove, and as the creature winged around the bowl Holt recognized it as a pigeon. Raising his left hand, pointing with three fingers, Sir Erik indicated the wall of the valley.

Getting its bearings, the bird abruptly soared over the cliffs, making a straight line toward the lowlands of the Tannyv Valley.

Mystified, Holt watched further. Something about that pointing gesture triggered a memory—and abruptly the truth came to him. He had seen the same gesture made by the warrior in Vanderton's marketplace—the black armored warrior who spoken to the silver merchant when Syssal Kipican had stolen the bracelet! Though he had not seen the fellow's face, the Daryman now felt quite certain that the man had been Sir Erik.

In fact, he'd said something about pigeons at the time, Holt remembered. Something he'd instructed the woman to do when the pigeon arrived.

Another shape moved in the shadowy doorway, emerging into the light. In the sunlight the tall, lanky form of a troll was clearly recognizable. The monster took a step toward Sir Erik.

Holt felt a flash of panic for the knight—forgetting for the moment that, since Sir Erik had been in the small hut, he must have known about the troll. His panic quickly faded into disbelief, and then a dour sense of betrayal, as the knight turned and spoke to the troll. Several other of the brutes came forward, gathered in an attentive circle around the suitor.

The Daryman shook his head in disbelief, unwilling to accept the implications. Yet the scene was clear: there was no rancor between the man and the trolls. In fact, the conclusion was completely inescapable.

Suitors Duel

Like the grotesque predators, Sir Erik Merriwell, Slayer of the Bull Troll, Grand Knight of
Rockeford, and Master of the Sword, was in reality
a servant of the dark force of Entropy.

14
Desperate Day

A rattle of stones in the gorge behind him pulled Holt's attention around, just in time to see a trio of gangly trolls lunging toward Old Thunder's hindquarters. One of the grotesque monsters barked loudly, the sound jarring through the still mountain air like a rockslide.

The narrow stone walls loomed too close for the big horse to turn around, even if there had been time for such a maneuver. Instead, Holt could see but one way to escape the immediate peril—he kicked his heels into Thunder's flanks, and the steed lunged forward, galloping out of the gorge and into the bowl-shaped valley. Sir Erik, hearing the commotion, turned and stared in astonishment as the young Daryman galloped into view. Immediately the knight shouted a command, and the trolls at the stone hut started scrambling through the snow, climbing toward Holt and Old Thunder.

The horse whinnied in pain as troll claws raked across his hindquarters. Lodestone Blade in hand, Holt twisted in the saddle and chopped at the nearest of the monsters, cutting its arm and drawing a surprised shriek of pain. All three of his pursuers dropped back, warily watching the gray-edged weapon.

Desperately, the Daryman considered his options. Pursued from behind while facing a dozen trolls and a knight before, Holt spurred the horse along the high slope above the hut, toward the cut on the opposite side of the valley.

Old Thunder pitched and leapt, bounding like a colt as he breasted the deep snow. The trolls behind fell back, floundering, while those climbing from below veered in pursuit. Sensing the man's intent, the monsters climbed through the powder in a frantic attempt to cut him off before he could reach the gap leading out of the vale.

Laying low along Thunder's broad withers, Holt stared in dismay, horrified by the speed of the climbing trolls. They sprang through the deep snow, bounding almost like rabbits as they clawed their way upward. Sir Erik, meanwhile, mounted his horse in grim silence and urged the steed along the track of his hideous lackeys.

Why would a man turn to Entropy? The question flitted through Holt's mind, arousing not so much mystification as outrage. Still, the answers would have to wait—the Daryman had far more pressing concerns.

The fastest of the trolls scrambled into the gap moments before Holt, turning to face the charging horse with bared fangs and hissing, growled threats. The other monsters were still a little way below as the Daryman urged Old Thunder forward. The horse reared, smashing down with his shaggy forehooves, crushing the troll to the ground. The beast reached up with a talon-studded paw, but a quick swipe of the Lodestone blade chopped the limb off at the wrist. Howling in pain, the troll scrambled to the side, while the horse and rider surged into the narrow gorge.

This rocky cut was deeper and slightly wider than the chasm Holt had ridden through before. For a moment the Daryman considered spinning about and making a stand, but he quickly discarded the idea. Even the Lodestone Blade could not balance the odds when he was pursued by so many trolls. And if he did hold the beasts at bay, Sir Erik, Master of the Sword, would be close behind.

Gray stone walls, jagged with cuts and ledges and draped with crystalline tendrils of ice, swept past him on either side. The gorge curved this way and that, so that rarely could he see more than a couple dozen feet before or behind. Even so, he could always see the pursuing trolls.

Barking, snapping, some of them even croaking like horrendous frogs, the creatures bounded after him with shocking speed. Their long, wiry legs propelled the beasts in a frantic sprint, and they didn't seem to grow tired. Old Thunder's nostrils flared, spewing gouts of steam as the gelding strained for more speed. Still holding his blade, Holt clung to the saddle and reins with his other hand. A fall would be fatal.

The floor of the gorge started to climb steeply, and the horse strained upward. Looking back, Holt saw the lead trolls springing after, and he slashed with his gray blade as several lunged for Thunder's streaming tail. Apparently the beasts feared that weapon, for they fell back with startling speed. Before him, Holt saw blue sky opening beyond the walls of the gorge—but he couldn't know what lay beyond.

Breasting a deep snowdrift at the top of the rise, Old Thunder skidded to a halt. A sweeping cliff plunged away from his feet, while narrow ledges, buried in drifts of soft snow, stretched to the right and left. Neither of the routes was wide enough for a horse and rider.

Whirling frantically, Thunder reared, kicking at the first two of the pursuing trolls and—temporarily, at least—holding the creatures at bay. More of the monsters scrambled into view behind the leaders, and Holt knew that Sir Erik couldn't be far behind.

Desperately the Daryman looked to each side. An attempt to ride along either ledge, he knew, would send both Old Thunder and himself plunging down the steep cliff. He didn't dare look below, but the fact that the bottom was far out of sight told him all that he needed to know. A person on foot, he saw, might be able to make it along the rocky shelf.

The heart-wrenching decision was obvious, yet he could not bring himself to make it. Old Thunder had carried him through many adventures, and the prospect of abandoning the horse in the face of these leering trolls brought him to the brink of total despair.

Yet if he stayed here, they would both be taken by the trolls or the knight—and this was an even more miserable prospect. He tried to convince himself that each of them would have a better chance alone. It was not so much that Holt feared for his life—though he very much wanted to live—but if he perished, the princess would have no way of knowing that one of her suitors was a traitorous servant of Entropy.

Holt slid from the saddle of the snorting horse. Just possibly, the riderless mount might be able to make his way along a ledge—it was all the Daryman could hope for.

"Good luck, old friend," he choked, clapping the horse on the flank. "I'm sorry!"

Old Thunder trotted away as Holt felt a rising wave of frustration rapidly build into fury. Savagely he chopped at the leading trolls, driving one the beasts back with several slashing cuts. The monster did not retreat very far, however, and—bolstered by the arrival of a half-dozen cronies—crouched menacingly, watching the Daryman with the impassive black holes of its eyes.

Now Sir Erik came into view, riding up behind the monsters and dismounting, his sword drawn. The creatures opened a path, allowing the knight to swagger forward. Holt had no choice but to retreat, or face certain death against the overwhelming odds.

The force of his rage overcame the Daryman's despair, drying his eyes and biting back the sobs in his throat as Holt turned along the narrowest of the ledges and started away from the gorge.

A troll lunged forward, reaching for the young farmer's foot as if it would pin Holt in place. Two quick cuts of the Lodestone blade dropped the beast and killed it, but three more trolls leapt over the corpse of their slain comrade before it grew still. Frantically the Daryman retreated along the shelf, chopping and slashing to hold the monsters just out of reach.

The ledge curved around a shoulder of the mountainside, and very quickly Holt moved out of sight of the gap where he had left Thunder. He could only hope that the horse had avoided the press of trolls, and soon even that flickering thought was driven away by the immediate challenge of survival.

It was only the Lodestone Blade, he knew, that gave him a slim chance of living. The trolls obviously feared the weapon, cringing away from his blows even when safely out of range. Once they learned the hard lesson that this weapon inflicted permanent wounds, they showed no overt enthusiasm for pressing the issue. Instead, the monsters pursued at a safe distance, forcing the Daryman steadily along the narrow shelf.

Kicking snow away below each footstep, Holt found that the ledge gradually climbed across the face of the cliff—and grew increasingly narrow the farther he moved from the gap. He was forced to clutch the rock wall with one hand while he brandished the sword with the other, moving around another jutting boulder that blocked his view along the mountainside.

He passed carefully around this obstacle, drove the nearest troll back with a sudden lunge, and then turned to look at his path. Despair grew again as he saw that, after another ten feet or so, the ledge ended. There was nothing but sheer cliff below and before him, and jagged, broken boulders sloping away overhead.

Still clutching his sword, Holt began to climb,

drawing himself up to a large shelf of rock, and then kicking his feet into narrow toeholds so that he could move even higher. A troll grasped at his foot and he turned to chop—but the monster pulled its hand away at the last moment.

The edge of the Lodestone Blade hacked into the mountainside with a numbing shock, and as Holt twisted to maintain his balance the hilt of the weapon slipped from his fingers. Crying out in frustration, he watched the sword slide down the rock and come to rest on the ledge below—where it was immediately surrounded by howling, yelping trolls.

Sir Erik, chortling with anticipated victory, came into view and quickly assessed the situation. Grinning broadly, he looked up at Holt, who was clinging with hands and feet to tiny holds in the rock, perhaps twenty feet overhead.

"So, Daryman—at last you achieve the heights you truly deserve!" His cruel laugh cut through Holt as savagely as any knife.

Yet the young farmer couldn't even pry a rock loose from the frozen cliff to use as a weapon.

"Kick it over the edge!" shouted the foul knight, gesturing toward the Lodestone Blade. The trolls, however, barked and spat, backing away from the weapon as if they still feared its power.

"Cowards! Curs!" snarled Erik, striding past the nearest trolls.

The knight's boot swept forward and Holt could

not suppress his gasp of dismay as he watched the precious weapon tumble outward, spinning over and over in the air as it plunged to the depths. In seconds it vanished from his view, still plummeting through the icy air.

"Thus I settle an old score, Daryman—one of many!" The knight shouted after him, and his voice twisted in fury.

"What score? You know I've never given you cause for this villainy!" Holt challenged. "Name the foul taint that lets you stand among these trolls, brings them to obey you!"

Erik shrugged, his anger settled—or held tightly in check. "They are convenient!" he snapped. "They help me achieve my ends."

"What ends make you my enemy?"

Abruptly the knight clapped his gloved hands together, seizing the fingertips of his left with the opposite hand. At the same time Holt realized that he had never seen those gloves come off—Sir Erik habitually wore them while riding and eating. Perhaps he slept in them as well, thought the Daryman.

With a furious gesture, the knight whipped off the left glove and shook a mangled hand at Holt.

"This is the debt you and your people owe me!" he screeched. "That sword sliced the fingers off this hand twenty years ago—and now my vengeance against it is complete.

Holt's mind reeled with thick, consuming horror.

He remembered his father's tale: the man who had helped the trolls plunder Oxvale, who had been wounded by Nowell!

In that sudden smash of revelation he understood that the mysterious human commander, the man responsible for his mother's murder, for the ruin of his village, now stood on the ledge below.

"Know this, Daryman!" taunted the knight. "When this quest is over, the meaningless contest disposed of, then shall I conquer Vanderthan with steel and with blood! There will be *no* survival for your pathetic village when I am through!"

The knight turned and stalked away while Holt clung to the mountainside. Tears of fury stung the Daryman's eyes as Sir Erik turned to watch his helpless adversary.

All Holt could do was continue upward, and this he did, scrambling with reckless haste to pull himself from one precarious handhold to another. As he climbed farther, he realized that he clung to the face of a narrow pinnacle of stone—a spire rising upward like a tower from the side of the mountain. Already the trolls leapt in pursuit, drawing themselves forward and up with tenacious savagery. Now that the Daryman was disarmed, the monsters showed no hesitation at all.

"I will leave you to the mercies of my servants," Erik called, leering up from the ledge. "It shall be my pleasure to return to the princess's side. Surely she will enjoy my company more, now that you won't be there to distract her."

"You're more of a monster than these trolls!" shouted Holt, again grasping fruitlessly for a rock, for *anything*, that he could use as a weapon.

"Perhaps—but I'm told it doesn't show," the knight replied, laughing heartily as he pulled the glove back onto his mangled hand. Holt saw that once again the fingers looked normal, albeit stiff and unmoving.

In moments the knight was out of sight.

The trolls climbed quickly, and Holt desperately scrambled to keep ahead of them. A loose rock broke beneath his foot and for a second he swung sickeningly over yawning space, clinging with both hands to a narrow crack in the cliff. The thought flitted through his mind—he could let go now and his torment would be mercifully over in a few seconds.

But such was not a choice he could make. Instead, grimly determined to fight until the last, he found another toehold and forced his way upward. Reaching a narrow chimney between two close-pressing faces of stone, he worked his way rapidly toward the top of the spire.

In a few minutes the crack opened out, and he reached the top. He crawled onto the narrow, irregular shelf of stone—no more than twelve feet in diameter—that capped the looming spire. A dazzling array of mountains swept away on all sides, but he took no time to admire the view—instead, he checked the cliffs on the opposite side, seeing trolls ascending there as well.

More than a dozen of the brutes crept toward him. There would be no escape from the attack. Instead, Holton Jaken, Daryman of Oxvale, kicked free several chunks of rocks. They would make only crude weapons, but he intended to sell his life at the highest cost possible.

15
Doomspire

Holt raised a rock, smashing it full into the face of the nearest troll. The brute, clawing for purchase on the flat top of the rocky spire, flinched backward as the stone struck between the ink-black eyes. Yet even under the fury of the blow the troll clung tightly to its perch, like some scale-coated crustacean sticking to a piling.

Furiously, the Daryman kicked loose another, heavier stone. Hefting it over his head in both hands, he hurled it with all the force he could muster. The missile crushed the monster's long, hooked nose, and the beast instinctively grabbed

171

at the wound with its wart-covered, long-fingered hands. Holt's boot followed the stone, and only then did the troll topple backward, twisting helplessly as it plummeted through the air.

The monster smashed against the stones far below, tumbling limply down the continuing steep slope until it finally halted, a bundle of broken bones and mangled flesh. Yet even before Holt tore his horrified eyes away, he saw the twisted limbs begin to straighten. The troll was too far away for him to see more, but Holt knew that the creature's wounds already healed. Soon it would be crawling inevitably, tirelessly upward, resuming the attack.

By the time it got here, Holt suspected, he would be dead.

Spinning to the other side of the narrow shelf, he saw another troll reaching its horrible claws over the top of the cliff. The Daryman stomped his heavy boot on the hand, forcing the troll to release its grip. When the other taloned hand lashed forward, he crushed those fingers as well. Hastily the monster withdrew out of sight, clinging to the cliff with three limbs while it waited for its hand to heal.

But now two more trolls were reaching upward, each from an opposite side of the narrow space. Again Holt knocked free a stone, using it to drive one of the trolls back. He picked up another rock and heaved it, but the troll on the far side ducked its head and the missile sailed harmlessly past.

The Daryman rushed the monster before it could raise its feet up to the top. Wobbling backward, the troll slashed with both foreclaws at the man, forcing Holt to skid to a halt. His boots slipped, and he sat down, hard, on the rocks—but before he noticed the pain he kicked outward with both feet, driving his heels into the troll's face and sending the monster tumbling to a temporary destruction on the lower slopes.

Still more hands, more horrible faces appeared around the rim of the small platform. In the background, Holt saw a bird winging closer, and imagined vultures and other carrion eaters gathering to the fight. He gritted his teeth in bitter irony, doubting strongly that the trolls would leave anything to the scavengers. The wretched thought almost caused him to laugh out loud.

In fact, Holt knew he had only a few more seconds to live. He rushed at a troll and even as the beast ducked away he sensed others of the brutes climbing higher. No less than three of the lanky monsters surged onto the cap of the spire, reaching out with horrible hands and hauling their kicking bodies upward.

Again that wide-winged bird caught his eye, and even in his desperate straits Holt felt a twinge of puzzlement. The creature clutched a stick of some kind in its claws, but surely it wasn't sweeping closer to build a nest! At the same time he realized that the bird was too stout, too short winged to be a vulture. Indeed, it looked startlingly out of place in these heights.

Abruptly recognition came, and with it a wave of gratitude. Sir Ira! As the owl soared closer Holt was overwhelmed with the knowledge that, at the very least, he would not die beyond the knowledge of his friends. The courageous bird was too small to aid him in his fight, but at least it could report the tale of his death.

Grimly, Holt remembered his vow—to make that death as costly as possible. Furiously he pulled stones free, hurling them to the right and the left in a doomed attempt to delay the inevitable.

"I say, Holton—catch!"

Sir Ira's voice, smooth and unflappable as ever, carried to him over the barking of the trolls and the swirling wind. In astonishment he looked up, for the first time realizing that the owl did not carry a mere stick.

It was the Lodestone Blade.

The owl flew over Holt's head, dropping the sword with perfect aim. Holt caught it by the hilt and in the same motion chopped through the body of the nearest troll. Spinning on his heel he hacked this way and that, quickly slaying three more of the beasts. Crouching low, using the bodies to conceal his sword from the rest of the trolls, he whirled and looked for the next attackers.

Three more of the monsters came clawing upward side by side. Waiting until their long, wiry necks were fully exposed, Holt sprang forward with upraised blade, removing the threat in three quick strikes. More of the trolls came from the opposite side, and he repeated the maneuver.

In short minutes, Holt stood alone, gasping for breath in the midst of a ring of slain trolls. Warily he looked to all sides, insuring that none of the creatures were lurking just below his lofty perch. Leaning out over the cliff, he spied the two trolls he'd knocked down earlier, resolutely climbing upward—although they were still far below. He had a few minutes, he knew, to catch his breath.

Sir Ira fluttered downward, coming to rest on the shoulder of a grotesquely killed troll. The owl preened his feathers a moment before looking at the Daryman with eyes that seemed uncharacteristically moist.

"Bit of a near shave, that," remarked Sir Ira, clearing his throat awkwardly. "Sorry I couldn't have gotten here sooner."

"You saved my life, old friend," Holt replied sincerely. "I think your timing was just about perfect."

"Now, what in all the spheres brings you to this high perch? You weren't thinking about building yourself a nest, were you?"

Holt described his adventurous day, from his initial quest in search of the presumably lost Sir Erik to the shocking discovery of the treacherous knight's true allegiance.

"He's probably making his way back to the others right now—they're in terrible danger!" the Daryman concluded.

"Right and wrong, I'd guess," the owl said patiently. "He no doubt is seeking to rejoin the princess and Prince Gallarath—but I suspect that he will make no overt or threatening move. At least, not yet."

"Why not?" Holt demanded, starting for the edge as he looked for the best route down from the pinnacle.

"Why, because he assumes you're dead, naturally," Sir Ira replied. "You're the only one who knows his true nature, and he's no doubt quite certain that he's removed you as a threat. He'll stick with his companions, perhaps until the goat is captured—or even until they return to Vanderthan. After all, his treachery can best be aided by keeping his identity concealed."

"You mean—he might even seek to win the contest? To *marry* Danis?" The thought sent a chill rippling along Holt's spine. "We've got to stop him!"

"And we will—but you have a couple more immediate concerns, if I recall correctly."

The Daryman remembered with chagrin that two trolls still climbed toward him. A quick check showed him that they were both very close, and for a short time he and the owl fell silent as they waited for these final foes to complete their approach.

Fortunately, the stupid creatures did not try to coordinate their assaults—perhaps because they fully expected to find their victorious comrades atop the towering spire. The first of the monsters gaped in surprise as it scrambled upward and found the multitude of troll corpses. The Lodestone Blade quickly removed that expression—and any other—from the grotesque features. In short minutes, the last of the brutes met the same fate as its fellows.

Only then did Holt begin the climb down, carefully moving from handhold to toehold, following the best route he could find in the steep face of the pillar. He was grateful that the precipice was scored with many cracks and ledges—nowhere was he forced to make any desperate leaps or frantic stretches.

Finally he reached the wide, lower ledge and hastened back to the place where he had been forced to abandon Old Thunder. His heart raced with hope as he saw great hoofprints along the ledge, which was slightly wider than the pathway he'd followed. Hurrying in the big horse's footsteps, he found that the rocky shelf curved gradually down toward the valley floor, continuing uninterrupted to the very foot of the wall. An incredible wave of relief swept through him as he saw from the tracks that Old Thunder had negotiated the entire distance without a fall.

Following along the trough left by the horse, the

Daryman made good time even through the deep snow of the valley floor. Old Thunder had apparently sensed the route back to the princess, Holt saw with gratitude.

Sir Ira soared and swooped overhead, winging on down the valley. Abruptly the owl dived, with a piercing hoot that carried to Holt's ears from better than a mile away. Sensing his companion's meaning, the Daryman jogged as quickly as he could, and in a short time came over a low lip in the descending valley floor.

There, in the midst of a great clearing in the snow, Old Thunder had pawed away the powdery cover and now nibbled at crusty lichens and low plants. With a joyful whinny, the horse looked up as Holt cried out. Kicking up his heels, Thunder galloped back along his tracks, nickering happily as the Daryman threw his arms around the broad and powerful neck.

"Come on, my friend," Holt whispered through his choking voice. "Let's find the princess—and get some measure of vengeance against that traitor!"

Perhaps the horse didn't understand the human's words—but nevertheless, the intent was clear. Holt leapt into the saddle and Old Thunder immediately turned, loping along as quickly as the deep snow would allow.

"You should fly ahead and warn them," the Daryman cried as Sir Ira soared next to him.

The owl spread his wings, settling to a gentle

landing on the horn of Holt's saddle. "Perhaps it would be best if we joined them together. I have a feeling that your arrival is going to give our knightly companion quite a jolt."

"I'd like to give him a jolt with *this!*" the Daryman declared, grimly placing a hand over the hilt of the Lodestone Blade.

"He's quite deserving of it, I'm sure," Sir Ira agreed. "But let's first settle for seeing that the princess is all right."

They rode in silence along a sweeping slope, gradually curving toward the vale where Holt had left Danis and Gallarath. Finally they crested the high ridge, and there, below them, Holt spied three riders. Even in the distance he knew that Sir Erik had rejoined Prince Gallarath and Danis. The three companions rode slowly toward a clump of white-frosted pines, apparently seeking a place to camp for the upcoming night.

Silently the Daryman urged his big horse forward, and Old Thunder breasted through deep snowdrifts, making his plunging way down toward the trio of riders. For several minutes the three companions below rode slowly onward, without noticing Holt's approach.

Finally Danis looked around, and Holt's heart swelled within him as he saw her golden hair shining in the late afternoon sun.

"Holt!" she cried, with an eager wave. She reined back on Lancer as the prince, too, pulled his mount to a halt.

Only Sir Erik reacted differently. The knight stared—even at this distance Holt could see Sir Erik's disbelief and astonishment. For a moment the man hesitated, as if debating whether to challenge the tale he knew the Daryman was about to reveal.

In another instant the knight made his decision. Before Holt could get close enough to shout a warning, Sir Erik put the spurs to his horse, galloping headlong toward the shelter of the woods. Danis and Gallarath looked in astonishment at their departing companion, but did not pursue. Instead, they turned back to welcome Holt—the princess with tears of relief in her eyes.

By the time the Daryman was close enough to speak, the treacherous knight had already vanished into the woods.

16
The Black Goat of Trollheight

"The vile, traitorous wretch! If he were here now, you can be sure he'd suffer the taste of my steel!" Prince Gallarath, his face flushed with outrage, raised his gleaming battle-axe in punctuation. Holt had just completed the tale of Sir Erik's treachery, during which the prince had quickly passed from skepticism to his current state of indignation.

"He's not," Danis said with a sigh. The princess was pale, obviously shaken by Holt's revelation. Now she looked at the trees that pressed close around them, as if wondering whether the villainous knight lurked behind the nearest branches. The pine grove they had approached earlier now encircled them, sheltering their night's camp.

"I don't think he'll trouble us in the immediate future," Holt observed. "After all, he got out of here pretty quickly. Though I do think Sir Ira should keep an aerial lookout while we march, and we should take turns holding a watch through the night."

The lower limbs of the pines offered many dry branches, while the upper portions of the trees formed a secure windbreak around them. In short order Holt had a crackling fire started, though the chilly portents of the day seemed to linger even in the face of the valiant flames.

"Why would Sir Erik go to all this trouble—what did he hope to gain?" Danis wondered, mystified.

"He placed you in terrible danger," Holt pointed out.

"The other suitors," Sir Ira noted. "Could it be that Erik had something to do with Lord Terragal's accident? Or Baron Durqueson's embarrassing predicament the night before we left Vanderton?"

"He was there!" Holt remembered. "He was the one who heard the noise from Baron Durqueson's room! And his horse was closest to Lord Terragal when the lord came so close to tumbling over the cliff."

"He wanted the Black Goat for himself—to win the contest!" Prince Gallarath declared indignantly.

"The contest!" Danis retorted bitterly. "It's a wild and pointless chase, dreamed up by my father in one of his less rational moments! What possible concern could the Black Goat of Trollheight be to the forces of Entropy?"

"The choice of the future king of Vanderthan could be *very* significant," Sir Ira pointed out. "Perhaps his mission was only that—to win the contest and insinuate himself into your father's grace."

"I—I don't think so," the princess demurred. "There's *got* to be something more!"

"The prophecy from the mirror?" Holt wondered. "Could it have been a trick to lure you here? Perhaps so that he could kill you?" The though sent chills of ice through his veins.

"Why hasn't he done so, then?" Danis replied.

Whatever that secret was, they could not discover it, though they discussed each possibility as the fire faded into embers. Gallarath volunteered to take the first watch, and as Danis and Holt settled into their bedrolls the matter was as much a mystery as it had been earlier.

"Perhaps when we find the Black Goat we'll get some answers," Holt said hopefully, before he drifted off to sleep.

"*If* we find it," Danis replied glumly.

When the prince awakened Holt for his turn at

the watch, the Daryman built up the fire and sat listening to the crackling of flames, wondering where Sir Erik had gone—and what his plans were. So deep were his musings that he didn't hear the sound in the woods until it had been repeated several times.

"*Baaaa!*"

Abruptly he sat upright. The bleating of the animal was unmistakable, and close. Blundering through the snow-draped branches, Holt all but stumbled over a dark shape. A pair of black horns glistened. He barely ducked away from the lunging charge of a dark-coated, four-legged creature.

"The Black Goat!" he gasped, seizing the animal around its shaggy neck. Suddenly docile, the goat followed him back to the fire, where it bleated plaintively.

Awakened by the commotion, Danis gasped as she saw the creature, which stood close to the coals. The inky pelt steamed from the heat, and the goat chewed contentedly, shrugging its shoulders as if to spread around the welcome warmth.

"*You* captured it?" demanded Gallarath, quickly springing to his feet and confronting Holt.

"I—well, no! It—it just followed me back here," the Daryman stammered, only slightly exaggerating.

"Oh, that's good," grunted the prince. He strode forward and grasped one of the animal's horns. "I pronounce the Black Goat captured—by myself!"

he declared proudly.

"Forget about that stupid contest!" Danis exploded. "We've got a traitor running around out here, and who knows what kind of trouble in the works—and all you can think about is a dumb animal!"

"It's not the sort of thing a woman should be expected to understand," Gallarath told Holt smugly.

The Daryman shook his head in amazement.

"At least we can head for home now," Danis declared. "The sky's getting light—let's saddle up the horses and get on our way."

After a cold breakfast they doused the remains of their fire beneath a pile of snow, mounted their horses, and turned again toward the lowlands. Gallarath threw a rope around the goat's neck and tied the other end to his saddle. Following in the tracks of the horses, the dark-cloaked animal lumbered along, still docile as the companions left the woods and started into the shallow, drift-filled valley. Sir Ira rode on Lancer's saddlehorn, accompanying the princess.

"The yetis' castle is that way," Holt remembered as they reached the edge of the next steplike descent.

"Perhaps we should avoid it on the way down," the prince observed. "After all, they seemed fond of this goat—they might not take kindly to our, er, finding it."

"Finding it they can't mind—it's our *taking* it that could put them in a bad mood," Danis declared sourly. The princess slouched in her saddle, glowering at her companions, occasionally fixing a glaring look on the Black Goat. The animal stared placidly back, still chewing absently.

Abruptly the First Daughter of Vanderthan sat upright in her saddle, her brow wrinkled by thought. "The prophecy from the mirror—it warned of some kind of drastic occurrence in the valley of the Black Goat! How is it that we just found the critter—and now it's coming along without a complaint?"

"The mirror was a gift from Sir Erik," Holt remembered. "Perhaps he wanted some excuse to get you up here."

"But *why?* He made no attack against me—though perhaps he would have if you hadn't returned when you did. Still . . ."

Danis's face suddenly grew pale, and she all but leapt from her saddle. Turning back to Lancer, she unlatched her saddlebag and reached frantically inside. His heart pounding, Holt understood what she looked for—and when he saw the bleak expression on her face, he knew what she had failed to find.

"The Crown of Vanderthan," the princess gasped, her voice a whisper of disbelief—and horror. "It's *gone!*" She shook her head miserably as tears welled in her eyes.

"Now, now," Gallarath said gently. "No matter how pretty the gold, how many gems stud the circle, a jeweled symbol of royalty can be replaced. Why, we have silversmiths in Rochester who, I'm quite certain, can easily render a replacement."

"Don't be a fool!" snapped Danis, her agitation pulling the cloak of tolerance off her shoulders. "The crown is an artifact of the immortals—it has powers that we can't even understand!"

The prince clapped shut his mouth, his jaw firmly set in displeasure and astonishment.

"She's right," Holt said—for once actually feeling sorry for the royal suitor. "The one who wears the crown can command unquestioning obedience from those around her—or him. It seems to make you invulnerable to attack. . . . It increases your senses, almost so that you can tell things are going to happen before—"

"It's an artifact that can make its wearer all-powerful—and at the same time completely removes any vestige of human conscience. It even makes you forget about your friends!" Danis declared bitterly. "These are all the reasons I put it away for safekeeping, so that it wouldn't fall into the wrong hands. Then, because of the prophecy from the mirror, when it seemed that I might need every resource to combat that dire threat, I brought it along."

"When the real threat was right here among us, disguised as a frien—well, a companion, in any event," Sir Ira summed up. "I say, that does make the quest for the goat seem rather superfluous, doesn't it?"

"I wish I had never heard of the accursed beast!" Danis said, regarding the black-pelted goat. The creature, contented as ever, regarded her while it continued to chew meditatively.

"Well, I don't know about that," Prince Gallarath said tentatively. "It still seems we'd best try to hurry the creature back to Vanderton. After all—"

"After all, we should leave it here!" Danis barked. "It doesn't belong to us, and the yeti will miss it. Untie it."

Gallarath seemed about to object, but one look at the expression on her face was enough to make him reconsider. Instead, the prince hemmed and hawed as he dismounted.

"I'll tell my father you caught it," Danis said, resignedly. "You win the contest—but let's not drag the poor animal all the way to Vanderton just to prove it!"

"But . . ." Prince Gallarath couldn't force himself to face the princess's wrath, but neither could he bring himself to free the animal.

"Perhaps we could, er, 'milk' her," Holt suggested, looking at the goat's bulging udder. "We could take some wine back—for the king—as further proof that we found the goat."

"Yes! Tellist asked us to do that—remember?" the princess noted.

"We could? That is, *yes!* We could!" the prince agreed, cheering up a little bit. He looked under the animal. "Does anyone know how to work these things?"

Suppressing a sigh of resignation, Holt dismounted. Danis handed him the ornate wineskin Tellist had given her, and he quickly filled it from the placid goat.

"Now—let's get back to Vanderthan as fast as possible. It makes me nervous knowing that traitor's somewhere around here—and that he has the crown," the Daryman announced.

"I agree," Danis said tiredly.

Even the prince, hefting the sloshing sack of wine, was forced to acknowledge the rightness of the suggestion.

With a plaintive bleat, the Black Goat watched them mount. Danis's flaring of temper had cooled a bit, and now she looked at the animal almost kindly. "You're free again," she said quietly. "Go back to your valley—and may you remain unvexed by questing humans!"

Prince Gallarath looked longingly at the animal, as if he wanted to throw out a loop and catch it again. One glance at Danis Vanderthan, however, dissuaded him of this impulse. He contented himself with a mumble of disgust before swinging back into his saddle. Holt mounted at the same time.

"No reason to avoid the yetis now. Let's take the fastest route out of these mountains," Danis said.

Nodding, Holt turned Old Thunder toward the slope that led into the vale of the Icekeep. The companions hadn't ridden for more than a dozen steps when the snowfield shivered around them and they found themselves in the midst of a ring of encircling snowmen. Obviously the creatures had been concealed here for some time, though the humans hadn't noticed them until the yetis chose to emerge.

Frostcrown and Winterbeard, side by side, stepped forward to confront the princess.

"You are a wise human," Frostcrown said, tipping his head in a respectful bow.

"Know that—if the Black Goat had remained your captive—you would never have left this valley alive," added Winterbeard cheerfully.

Gulping, Holt looked at the solid ring of snow creatures, and knew that they would not have been able to escape—even if they had wanted to fight the hulking, shaggy beings. He realized that it was true good fortune that Danis had decided to release the animal—or had it been, perhaps, wisdom?

"The goat is a being of the heights—as are you yeti," the princess declared solemnly. "Though she may be worth much in the human realms, it would have been wrong to remove her from these mountains. Watch her well, my friends."

"Aye . . . friend," Frostcrown said, as if tasting the word and finding it palatable.

Suitors Duel

"Indeed—and if ever you return, know that you will be welcome in the Trollheights," added Winter-beard.

Even Gallarath seemed impressed, nodding respectfully to the shaggy yetis as the three riders filed past. Sir Ira swirled and soared overhead, hooting cheerily, as the humans started back toward the lowlands.

Hours later, when they had crossed to the lip of the lower valley, Holt looked back at the high horizon. He barely saw the tiny figures there, but knew that the yetis were still watching them. As the riders dropped out of sight, the Daryman waved. Two of the distant yetis raised their hands in response.

The last things he saw as they rode downward from the heights were those two burly figures, watching motionlessly, hands raised in a gesture of friendship and farewell.

18
Distant Menace

Winding down the slopes of the Trollheights, the companions leaned back in their saddles. They were grateful to leave the deep snowfields behind, but all the same were blanketed by a sense of gloom, loss, and failure. Holt, mounted on Old Thunder, led the way, with Danis behind and the prince trailing in the rear. Sir Ira soared overhead, relishing the warmer air of these lower elevations.

If Gallarath fully understood the nature of their escape from the yetis' wrath, he made no mention of the fact. Instead, he sulked, unhappy that his black-coated prize had been left in the mountains.

The horses, crossing a smooth, sunward-facing slope, clopped through snow no more than a few inches deep. Spared from the necessity of following in Thunder's deep tracks, Danis pulled Lancer even with the Daryman. The princess rode in silence, her head down, the sodden tangle of her hair concealing her face from Holt.

The Daryman reflected, bitterly, that for once he had the chance to talk to her without the interference of any pestering suitors—and their mood was too bleak for any kind of pleasant conversation.

"How could I have been so *stupid?*" Danis moaned, suddenly raising her head and fixing Holt with a glare that demanded he answer—but warned him that his answer had better be very carefully phrased.

Wisely, he said nothing.

"I *knew* how precious the crown was—how important it was to make certain it stayed out of the wrong hands! So what do I do—I take it out of the castle, where the wrong hands could snatch it! Holt—what are we going to do?"

He shook his head miserably, though a tiny corner of his heart flickered. Danis had said what are *we* going to do! She knew that she could count on him for all the help he could offer. Unfortunately, that seemed like precious little comfort at the moment.

"I—I could chase Sir Erik to Rockeford," he suggested. "Perhaps I could steal it back. . . ." The

suggestion sounded ridiculous even as it left his
lips.

"It's the *Crown of Vanderthan!*" Danis snapped.
"You, better than any other man, understand its
powers. If Erik is wearing it, he'll probably know
you're coming by the time you cross the border of
his realm." Her tone softened slightly. "It was a
brave suggestion, but it just wouldn't work."

"I know," he agreed unhappily. The Daryman
thought fleetingly of Fenrald Falwhak, missing his
friend more than ever since the hearty dwarf's
departure. He looked across the sweeping slope of
the mountain range, knowing that Graywall lay
somewhere in the distance. He could almost imagine his friend's gruff voice calling out to them, ask-
ing if all was well.

"Did you know that's the border of Rockeford—
that scoundrel's realm?" Gallarath muttered,
drawing even with Danis and Holt. Surprised,
the Daryman's eye followed the prince's pointing
finger.

A swath of rolling ground stretched away, beyond the silvery ribbon of the Tannyv River. The
nearer bank of the great waterway was a sweep of
forest and meadow, untrammeled by roadways or
towns; the far bank, however, was dotted with several sprawling communities, and pale lines that
could only be wide highways linked them in a web-
like network.

"He might be back there already—with the

crown," Danis said bitterly.

In silence the three riders continued along the ridge. By unspoken consent they halted their descent, instead moving along the side hill steadily closer to Rockeford. What they hoped to see there Holt couldn't imagine—it was more frustrating than anything else to look at that vast realm and imagine the villainous Sir Erik reaching safety. And that was even before the Daryman allowed himself to worry what kind of trouble the ignoble knight would be able to wreak with that potent immortal artifact.

"I say—there seems to be a bit of activity along that highway," Sir Ira remarked, spiraling low about the riders.

Holt squinted, but could make out nothing beyond the brownish course of the road along the far river bank.

"We'd best get a bit closer," the owl suggested, his voice unusually somber. "I'll take a look from the air—you keep riding."

Not for another half hour could the humans discern what Sir Ira had seen. To Holt, the strip of riverside road looked much like any other, except that perhaps its color was a trifle darker. Still, that could be explained as a different type of soil, or because the low ground was saturated with water. Yet gradually the strip seemed more and more odd. There was a strangeness to it that came to him in a flash.

"The road seems to be moving," he said, wonderingly. The long ribbon of darkness inched along the highway, its movement barely perceptible to the distant observers.

Finally it was Gallarath who gave words to their silent, fearful speculation. "That's an army on the march."

Holt wanted to hear a trace of doubt in the prince's voice, but none was present. Gallarath had made the only possible explanation for the distant phenomenon.

"The Army of Rockeford, on the march down the Tannyv Valley." The prince shook his head in wonder. "It takes time to put a force like that together —this must have been part of his plan all along."

"It's marching on Vanderthan!" Danis gasped.

"And Oxvale," Holt added grimly.

"We've *got* to get home!" the princess declared, pulling on Lancer's reins to wheel the fleet charger through a half circle. Her next cry of alarm pulled Holt's eyes to the rear.

The trolls were barely a hundred paces away and closing fast. Several dozen of the ugly, gangly creatures swept down from the ridgecrest in a horrid charge. Advancing in a broad, enclosing arc that threatened quickly to encircle the companions, the monsters hissed and barked.

"Downhill!" shouted Holt, jabbing his heels into Old Thunder's flanks. Even before his kick the big gelding lunged, galloping at breakneck speed

across the shallow snowfield. Lancer and Gallarath's charger, likewise, raced away from the
threat.

Tears stung Holt's eyes as the wind whipped
past his skin—suddenly it seemed much colder
than it had a moment before. He felt the Lodestone
Blade at his side, but knew that there were too
many of the creatures to fight. If they were trapped
they would battle to the last, but as long as they
had the slightest prospect of escape they must flee.

"Look!" cried Danis, her voice shrill with alarm.
She pointed below and to the left, where another
company of trolls—twice as many as in the first
group—now raced around the shoulder of the
flanking mountain. The new arrivals loped along
the mountainside, often using hands as well as
feet for speed and balance.

Continuing straight downhill, the Daryman
knew, would inevitably bring them against the
bank of the Tannyv. This close to the mountains
the river was ice-choked, but streams of clear
water showed through the floes. Too, the near bank
plunged away in a steep bluff, showing no promise
of any negotiable descent.

Feeling trapped, Holt veered toward the right,
trying to draw away from both of the snarling
bands. The horses stretched into full gallop, crossing the snowy ground at an angle to the slope,
dropping slightly as the companions approached a
looming shoulder of cliff. Fortunately, a band of

smooth ground extended around the base of the cliff—just above the drop-off to the river.

Then Holt's heart sank as he sensed movement along that strip of passable terrain. Dozens of trolls came into view, surging toward the companions, blocking off their last chance of escape.

"Against the cliff!" shouted the prince. "We'll stand them off with our backs to the wall!"

"We can't stop running—as soon as we let them corner us we're doomed!" the Daryman protested. He looked to the right, groaning as he saw that the charging trolls above had strung into a long line. The brutes could quickly converge, he knew, if the companions slowed their pace to climb uphill.

"Charge them—straight ahead!" cried Danis, drawing her silvery sword and waving it over Lancer's head. The black charger lowered his neck and raced across the smooth ground. Still some distance away, the trolls before them ceased their loping advance and spread into a long line, completely blocking the gap between churning river and sheer, rising cliff.

A sound like thunder cracked through the air, echoing from the heights across the river, rumbling in Holt's chest with a formidable, undeniable power.

"Stop!" he shouted, hauling backward on Old Thunder's reins. A quick look behind showed him that they had several minutes before their pursuers could close the gap.

Suitors Duel

Danis and Gallarath sensed his unease, for they, too, stopped as quickly as possible.

"Look out—up above!" Sir Ira shouted, wheeling past the companions, back along their tracks.

Looking upward, Holt gaped in disbelief as a great shelf of ice and snow broke from the top of the cliff, surging down in a tumbling cascade of white. The avalanche swept boulders and tree trunks into its embrace, picking up speed, smashing across the steep ground with terrific force.

Even before the riders spurred their mounts, the horses turned and fled along their tracks. They were near the fringe of the slide, and Holt saw that they just might get free before it struck the base of the cliff.

The trolls that had blocked their path, however, were not so lucky—the avalanche thundered downward, straight toward their compact line. Some of the monsters broke forward while others fled to the rear. None would even reach the fringes of the slide.

The ground shuddered underneath the horses' hooves. Old Thunder stumbled for a heart-stopping moment but smoothly resumed his strides. Holt didn't look behind, even when he felt a spray of ice-crystals against his back. Chunks of crusted snow bounced past, but none of the boulder-sized blocks struck the companions or their mounts. Explosions of sound rocked the air, sweeping across them, threatening to smash them to the ground.

Finally the sounds of chaos settled and the trio wasted no time halting their flight—which had carried them perilously closer to the pursuing trolls. A cloud of snow billowed like smoke through the air, and a few rocks clattered down the cliff in the wake of the slide, but the danger seemed to be over.

Wheeling about, Holt was elated to see not a single living troll amid the wreckage of the avalanche. Some of the icy cascade had spilled all the way across the narrow shelf, tumbling into the river, but most of it lay strewn in irregular heaps across the ground.

What could have caused such fortuitous destruction? Only then did the Daryman think of looking upward. "Frostcrown! Winterbeard!" He pointed to a row of tiny figures, barely visible at the top of the cliff. Two of them raised their hands, waving.

Exclaiming in joy, Danis waved frantically, while Gallarath probed forward, looking for a path through the wreckage left by the avalanche. "Looks okay here, closer to the edge," he said cautiously.

Barks and howls of savage frustration rose from the two bands of trolls behind them as the companions started along the top of the bluff. Below, the ice-choked waters of the Tannyv slid past, while above the gray cliff yawned imperious and uncaring.

In places across the snowfield the limb or head of a troll protruded from the snow. Already these body parts twitched with returning vitality. Yet the weight of crushing snow was sufficient to hold the monsters immobile—at least while the companions made their way across the rough ground.

Once beyond, they gave the horses free rein, and the steeds once again raced along the top of the bluff, slowly drawing away from the pursuing trolls.

"With a little luck, we can outdistance them up the river," Holt shouted over the wind of the ride. "Then find a place to cross—oh, no!"

Gallarath cursed loudly and Danis groaned in dismay as they galloped around the far side of the looming cliff. Their path was clear for perhaps another mile, but then an encircling wall of rock dropped from the heights to completely block any path of escape—at least, any overland route. Black, stony cliffs rose from the river's edge to merge into the mountainous summits above.

"This way!" A voice came from above as Sir Ira soared past, flapping desperately to turn away from the looming cliff. "I'm not sure what the ground is like—but there *might* be a way for you to get down!"

Holt looked despairingly at the rumbling torrent of the High Tannyv. Huge floes of ice pocked the surface, drifting downstream. These islands of frost were surrounded by stretches of dark, roiling water.

"Here's a gully—we might be able to get down to

the bank," the Daryman suggested, pointing to a narrow cut in the lip of the riverside bluff.

"We'll break our necks!" Gallarath objected after a quick look at the steep drop.

"At least we'll have a *chance!*" Danis announced, urging Lancer into the steeply sloping ravine. Swiftly she dismounted, leading the skittery horse by the bridle. Holt quickly followed suit.

After a look at the trolls—now closing with renewed fury—the muttering prince slid to the ground and led his own horse after the others. The route was steep, but at least they didn't encounter any clifflike dropoffs. In a few minutes they had reached the bank of the broad, turbulent Tannyv.

"Up here!" Holt suggested, gesturing along the ice-choked shoreline. He looked upward, catching a momentary glimpse of many trolls tumbling and sliding down the ravine in pursuit. Leaving Old Thunder for a moment, the Daryman darted across the treacherous, slick surface of the bank, stepping onto a flat slab of ice that extended outward into the current. A narrow neck connected the ice to the shore. Looking downward, Holt saw that the ice was close to a foot thick.

"Bring the horses out here!" he shouted. "We might be able to break it loose!"

"Are you *crazy*?" demanded the prince, shaking his head in refusal—a refusal that lasted only until Danis led Lancer and Old Thunder out to the Daryman's side.

Holt drew his sword and began to chop at the thinner ice connecting this float to the shoreline. By the time Gallarath had scrambled aboard their impromptu raft, he had chiseled a great deal of frost away.

The prince lent a hand as numerous trolls spilled from the bottom of the ravine. With howls of outrage the monsters galloped toward them.

A sharp *crack* split the air as the current tugged the weakened ice floe away from shore. The lead trolls skidded to a halt at the edge of the ice, shaking their fists, spitting, and yowling after the three humans.

Holt staggered backward, slumping with disbelief and weakness as the shoreline receded. The current pulled the ice floe along, and swiftly the rapid waters of the High Tannyv pitched and churned to all sides of them.

19
River of Ice and Steel

The river was at least a hundred paces wide, not terribly deep—but deep enough. Rapids pitched over boulders, and currents eddied through dips and over submerged obstacles. High bluffs flowed past on the left bank, while an expanse of forest pressed close to the Tannyv on the right. Neither fact was particularly relevant, Holt realized, since they could do nothing to control the direction of their movement.

The wide ice floe wheeled gracefully in the center of the tumbling river. Holt grew dizzy as he constantly stepped sideways, keeping his eyes on the expanse of the Tannyv before them.

Their float jostled into other ice floes, often with brutal force. Frequently stumps or entire tree trunks would nudge one side or the other of their emergency raft.

More distressing than the jolting was the fact that each of these collisions chipped away a small portion of the icy platform. Too, as they floated toward warmer climes, Holt knew that melting would rapidly reduce the size of their frozen craft.

"Brace yourselves," Danis warned as a looming iceberg surged against them. The ice floe cracked and shifted, and the three companions scrambled with their horses to the middle of the remaining chunk.

"It's pushing us toward the far shore," Holt observed hopefully. They began wheeling in the opposite direction, but now the current eddied around a large crag of rock in the center of the stream. They swept to the right; the floe pitched and rocked into a tumbling chute of rapids.

"Hang on!" cried the prince, kneeling and clutching the reins of his panicking horse.

"To what?" Holt demanded, nevertheless doing the same. Old Thunder's broad hooves remained firmly placed on the slippery surface, and even when the raft surged violently to the side the big horse didn't lose his footing.

"Look—we're running toward that spit of land!" Danis cried, pointing to a forested peninsula that jutted into the river. Deep waters eddied behind the barrier, and for a moment the raft slipped out of the current, slowly wheeling toward shore. With a gentle bump, one portion of the ice met the river bottom, a few feet from dry land.

"Go—let's get off here!" urged Holt. His companions needed no persuasion as each of the humans slipped and stumbled into the knee-deep water, splashing frantically toward shore. The Daryman released Old Thunder's reins and waded to the muddy bank on his own. As he had expected, the horse, not wanting to be left behind, jumped after. Thunder's hooves slipped down the bank, showered cascades of spray as the big animal churned and labored his way upward, finally reaching dry ground.

Quickly Danis and Gallarath joined him, their own chargers leaping gracefully after. In another moment a finger of current reached into the eddy and tugged at the ice floe. Slowly, reluctantly, the slab of frost twisted back into the current, bucking and cracking as it flowed out of sight downriver.

"Nice bit of an escape," Sir Ira remarked from the branches of a nearby tree. "Now, does anyone know where we are?"

"On the other side of the river from the trolls," Holt declared. "I'd say that's the most important thing."

"Quite," agreed the owl. Preening wing feathers with his stubby beak, Sir Ira stretched and nodded.

"This should be the Greenbriar Forest," Prince Gallarath said hesitantly. "My kingdom lies on the far side of the wood."

"Is it close to here?" asked Danis.

"Actually, no. The forest is huge. For the most part, it's wilderness, though some human woodsmen labor near the fringes on the far side. As far as I know, the great bulk of the woodland is unexplored."

"I'll settle for that," Holt said sincerely. Stepping between some broad, mossy tree trunks, he looked around. "The trees are so high that they choke out most of the underbrush. We'll have no difficulty walking along the forest floor."

"Let's get going," Danis urged. "If we keep the river in sight, we'll know that we're following the Tannyv valley—and that will take us to Vanderthan." She turned to Holt, her expression pleading. "Do you think we can get back home in time to warn them of Sir Erik's army?"

"I'd think the three of us can travel faster than a large force," the Daryman guessed—though he had no experience with armies. "Especially since we've all got horses."

"I say. If worst comes to worst, I can always fly ahead with the news—I'd hate to leave you folks in the thick of the forest, though," Sir Ira noted.

Suitors Duel

"Let's stick together as long as possible," Holt agreed. Perhaps it was just his imagination, but something about the heavy, gnarled trunks around them, the deep shadows, and the eerie stillness made him uneasy. Apparently his companions shared the feeling, for they wasted no time in mounting their horses and started along the river-bank.

Holton Jaken had spent many enjoyable days in the woods around Oxvale. The Knollbarren wilderness, also heavily wooded, had been the scene of many of his extensive hunts and youthful explorations. Yet never in all those travels had he seen a woodland that seemed so ancient, so all-encompassing, as the place Gallarath called the Greenbriar Forest.

Some of the trees were so huge that, had the three of them joined hands, they still would not have been able to encircle the gnarled boles. Moss draped from many of the overhanging limbs, while knot-holes and twisted branches gave the unsettling impression of facial expressions or secret hiding places. The leaves overhead, tinged with autumn colors, were so thick that little sunlight reached the forest floor. Though this contributed to the gloomy aura, Holt knew that they had these same shadows to thank for the relative ease of travel.

Indeed, the ground was for the most part a smooth, grassy expanse, occasionally marred by a rotted limb, twisted root, or lichen-encrusted boulder. The horses plodded easily along, the waters of the Tannyv sparkling incongruously just to their left. Sir Ira soared and swooped around, keeping his sharp eyes alert for danger.

For two days of urgent travel they saw no sign of any creatures, other than the squirrels, rabbits, and birds that inhabited any typical woodland. Indeed, except for the haste of their riding—which put them on the trail from dawn until dusk every day—they might have enjoyed their pastoral surroundings. The army across the river remained screened from view, but none of them doubted that it continued its inexorable advance. At night they found sheltered hollows, and camped around the comfort of a smokeless, hardwood fire.

Midway through their third day in the wood, Holt was beginning to wonder if this forest went on forever. They had found no clearing, not even the tiniest meadow, in their miles of riding. If not for the comforting presence of the river on their flank, he wouldn't have known if they were riding around in circles.

The Daryman's mind was occupied with these thoughts when an incongruous sound reached his ear. Pulling Old Thunder to a halt, he listened carefully and heard it again—a hard, thunking sound that reverberated through the trees with unnatural force. When it was repeated again and again, he knew it could only be one thing.

"Someone's chopping wood near here," he announced as his companions gave him puzzled looks. "It's coming from somewhere up ahead."

"Let's see who it is," Danis suggested.

Riding with a little more caution than previously, the three companions advanced through the woods toward the rhythmic sounds of the chopping. Gliding nearby, Sir Ira kept pace, swooping from limb to limb in silence. Shortly the riders came around the trunk of a massive tree, seeing the back of a white-haired man as the fellow hoisted a sturdy axe and brought it down into a stump, splitting the heavy log into two pieces.

"Ho, woodsman," Prince Gallarath said, drawing a startled oath from the fellow. The white-haired axeman whirled in shock, blinking his watery eyes in consternation at the three riders.

"What? Eh? Who's that?" he demanded in a crotchety voice, his white beard quivering with surprise—or suspicion.

As he studied the man, Holt was surprised that such a frail person could heft the heavy axe. His arms and legs were sticklike, and his beard of flowing white framed a wrinkled, wizened face. The hair on his scalp was wispy, and his knees all but knocked together as he regarded the trio.

"This is none other than Princess Danis, First Daughter of Vanderthan!" Gallarath announced with a gesture toward the woman. "And I am Prince Gallarath, heir to the throne of Rochester!"

"Eh? And you?" demanded the old fellow, squinting at Holt.

"I'm a Daryman of Oxvale," he replied, bowing his head stiffly.

"Pretty rich company for the back woods," remarked the fellow, sitting on a stump and wiping the sweat from his brow. "Whyn't you come down off them horses and chat a bit?"

The prince spoke sharply. "We're on an urgent—"

"It might not hurt to rest—and perhaps we can learn a little more about what's going on," Danis declared, smoothly dismounting. "And who might you be, sir?" she inquired as the prince and the Daryman slid from their own saddles.

"A simple denizen of these woods, trying to make an honest living," the man declared, with a wink at Holt. "But what is the task that drives you through the forest with such urgency?"

"Know you that the army of Rockeford is on the march?" demanded Gallarath. "Even now they file down the far bank of the Tannyv, bound for plunder and war."

"I had heard of this—even trolls, it is said, march under the banner of the Black Knight."

"The Black Knight?" Danis raised her eyebrows, trying to conceal the tremor in her voice.

"It is said that this army is led by a warrior who bears a mighty sword, and would make himself king of every realm in the valley."

"Sir Erik!" Holt blurted.

"Where are we in the Greenbriar Forest?" Galla-rath asked. "How far to the edge of the woods?"

"Well, that depends. Along the river here, another day's ride will take you to the border of Vander-than. If you cut away from the river, though—" here the man pointed into the depths of the wood "—barely a few hours will take you into the high moors. You'll find yourself on the border between Bedford and Rochester."

Holt saw a flash of silver when the woodsman pointed. The sparkle came from the fellow's wrist where, incongruously, he wore a heavy silver bracelet. As soon as he dropped his arm, the circlet was covered by his sleeve.

But that glimpse was sufficient for the Dary-man to recognize the ring of silvery metal. He lunged forward and grasped the man by the wrist. Though the woodsman pulled away with surpris-ing strength, Holt lifted the sleeve to reveal the bracelet—the object that was identical in every respect to the gleaming circlet lost and regained by Syssal Kipican.

"What thievery is this?" demanded the Dary-man. "Explain how you came by such a treasure! Admit it, man—you stole it. It is the treasured property of one who befriended me."

With a shy smile, the woodsman reached out and unclipped the bracelet. As it fell from his wrist, so did the fellow's complete appearance drop away— the white hair and beard, the tattered clothes, the stooped and frail body all vanished. In its place stood none other than the elven thief himself!

"Syssal!" gasped Holton, stepping backward in shock.

"I see that you noticed my bracelet of disguise," declared the elf with a smile. Syssal's large eyes sparkled; the golden strands of his hair seemed to glow in the semi-shadow of the forest floor. A tunic of shimmering silk swung gracefully from his shoulders. "And I appreciate that you remember me fondly."

"What's going on?" demanded Prince Gallarath, blinking and looking behind himself, as if he suspected that the woodsman had made some kind of remarkable escape.

The elf clapped the bracelet over his wrist again, and the three humans gasped as they found themselves facing a curvaceous dwarven woman. The bracelet came off, and they saw Syssal Kipican again.

"This is how I made my way around the castle," the elf admitted to Holt. "But it really *has* been in my family for centuries, as I told you."

"Of course!" Holt couldn't help but laugh. "And you stole it from that peddler?"

" 'That peddler' is none other than a witch of Entropy," the elf declared ominously. "I wasn't certain at first, but from what I have learned since I know this to be true. I'm aware of some other things, too—that's why I awaited you here."

"How did you know we were coming?" Holt asked, mystified.

"The heart of Greenbriar is *our* wood," the elf said—with a meaningful look at the prince. "We elves make certain to know what transpires here —and who travels here." Syssal turned to Sir Ira, who sat sagely on a shaded limb, blinking and preening like any anonymous owl. "Welcome to the forest, Wise One. It has been a long time since one of the Hsiao has graced our woodland."

"Oh, er, delighted, I'm sure," said Sir Ira, flustered at the elf's ready identification.

"That witch in the marketplace was in league with Sir Erik!" Holt remembered. "He was the one who told her . . . something." He groaned in frustration, suspecting that the message might prove terribly important. "She was to 'lift the bar when the white dove flies'. . . something like that! I can't remember the exact words!"

"It sounds like a plan to open the castle gates," Danis said, horrified. "If the town is attacked and Sir Erik's army reaches the palace walls—the whole defense could collapse!"

"I say. Perhaps it's time for me to fly ahead," Sir Ira remarked with a blink of his eyes. "I could carry an alarm that would set the guards on alert, at the very least."

"And Father could gather his forces," Danis added, her tone despairing. "His army is small, but at least they'll be ready."

"I, er that is, Rochester has a sturdy force of men-at-arms," Prince Gallarath offered. "If I take the inland road, I should be able to muster a respectable force. It would take a little time—but I should be able to reach the border of your father's realm in perhaps four days."

Danis turned to the prince, her eyes warm with gratitude. "Thank you," she said. "Please make all haste."

"What about the elves?" Holt said. "Surely this army is a threat to your wood! Can you send warriors to help bring the invasion to a halt?"

Syssal looked genuinely sad. "I wish you well in your battle—but this is a human matter. I cannot command my fighters to sacrifice blood and lives in your cause."

A graceful figure emerged from behind a nearby tree, startling Holt with his nearly magical arrival. The fellow was a golden-haired elf, though dressed in a brown robe much plainer than Syssal's silken garb.

"Forgive my intrusion, Eminence," the newcomer said, bowing low to Syssal Kipican. The Daryman gaped at the elven thief, astonished to see him addressed in such a fashion. "But I bring news of the menace."

"Speak, Pallithan," Syssal commanded.

"The Black Knight's army has altered course. They halt at the riverbank a few miles from here. They have begun to fell many trees."

"Do you suspect . . . ?" The elven chieftain's question remained unfinished, but heavy with apprehension.

"Yes, Lord," replied the scout. "I fear that they are making rafts. Their intention must be to cross the river."

"And bring their war to Greenbriar," Syssal added grimly. He turned to look at the humans. "It would seem that we're about to become allies, after all."

20
Tide of Entropy

Sir Ira winged toward Vanderthan with what he normally would have considered unseemly haste. Prince Gallarath departed, too, after securing good directions to Rochester from Syssal Kipican. He promised to do his best to bring his army to the edge of the forest by the time four or five days passed.

Holt, expecting that Syssal Kipican would immediately start for the site of Erik's river-crossing, was surprised when the elf settled down to build a small fire and roast several pieces of venison. Pallithan, the scout, gathered a number of greens and produced a loaf of hard bread from his backpack.

"Shouldn't we get going—see their army for ourselves?" the Daryman asked, though his stomach rumbled at the scent of the grilling meat.

"Elven eyes do their best seeing after dark," Syssal replied. "We might as well travel on full stomachs. Besides, Pallithan tells me that they're all on the far side of the river. It will take some time for them to prepare for the crossing."

Dusk settled around them as Syssal and Pallithan finally led Danis and Holt toward the riverbank. More elves appeared behind them, seemingly emerging from the tree trunks themselves. Each of these golden-haired woodsmen carried a bow and wore a quiver full of arrows. Their arrival was heartening, but by sunset there were still no more than two dozen of them—a force that could be no more than a minor nuisance to the Army of Rockeford.

"There'll be more as the days go by," Syssal remarked. "But our people are scattered the length and breadth of Greenbriar—it will take some time for a force to gather."

Finally they reached the bank, where the surprisingly placid waters of the Tannyv sparkled under the pale starlight. Across the river they saw campfires too numerous to count, apparently extending for a mile or more along the far bank. The steady chopping of axes was a regular cadence in the background, and Holt knew that Erik's warriors were felling dozens, perhaps hundreds of trees.

"They stopped here this morning," Pallithan explained. "It would seem that they plan on building rafts, perhaps making a ferry."

"They've picked a good spot for it," Syssal agreed grimly. "Above and below here the river is rapid and rough, but for this stretch the current is slow, the surface placid."

"What can we do to stop them?" Holt wanted to know, clenching his fists in frustration.

"Nothing—for now," Syssal declared. "But let's see what happens tomorrow."

With that unsatisfying course of action before them, Holt and the princess found places to spread their bedrolls. All through the night the chopping of the woodcutters, punctuated by the occasional crash of a falling tree, disturbed the peace of the forest.

Sir Erik's army continued its preparations during the following day and night, collecting huge logs, proceeding with the building of a massive raft. Infuriated, Holt and Danis could only observe their enemies' activities, helpless to do anything to stop the steady work. A hundred or more times during the day, they hoped aloud that Prince Gallarath and Sir Ira would be able to muster a defensive force in time.

Securely hidden in the dense woods atop a riverside bluff, the two humans and Syssal Kipican watched while Erik's troops lashed their logs into a massive raft on the far side of the mighty Tannyv. The biggest trees along the riverbank had been felled for a great distance in each direction, and teams of laboring oxen hauled these back to the building site. That process continued by torchlight well into the night.

Dawn revealed a massive raft secured to the shoreline, partially obscured by morning mist. At least a hundred trolls climbed aboard and began poling away from shore. The raft floated into the river, though it remained attached by a heavy rope to the far bank. Pushing furiously on their long, hand-held shafts, the trolls propelled the barge through the current, which—as Syssal had told them—was much more placid here than in other places.

"Can we meet them at the bank—try to hold them off?" Holt asked as he and Syssal crept closer for a look.

The elf shrugged in regret. "I have some fifty archers here now. We can shower those trolls with arrows until our quivers are empty, but they'll pull them out like pesky thorns and throw them in the river. Not much sense in making giant pincushions out of the trolls for a few minutes, when those same arrows might be used to good effect against humans later."

Holt wanted to argue, but he could see that the

elf made sense—they might as well shoot their missiles directly into the river, for all the effect they would have on the hideous trolls.

After two hours, the monsters reached the near bank, where they secured the other end of the massive rope. Leaving a great number of trolls to guard their ferry landing, a few of the brutes then hauled the raft back over the river, following the course of their heavy line. A large company of spear-bearing footmen were the next invaders to cross. They started gradually, pulling along the rope, and Holt guessed that nearly three hundred men would soon arrive on the once-pastoral bank of Greenbriar.

At the same time, the trolls guarding the ferry landing spread into the nearby woods—almost as if they had sensed the presence of Syssal's elves. The archers who had tried to infiltrate the woods around the camp were forced to fall back to save their lives, leaving them out of range of the bank.

"We have to do *something!*" Holt groaned, shaking his head.

"What do you suggest?" Syssal asked sincerely.

"Could we cut the rope?" the Daryman wondered.

"It's pretty well guarded . . . here at the end, anyway."

An idea began to form in Holt's mind. "Can elves swim?" he wondered.

"Like fish," Syssal replied, shrewdly looking at

the Daryman.

"So can I. There might be a way to slow them up a bit, after all. Here's my idea. . . ."

* * * * *

Two hours later, a company of human footmen landed and the raft started back to the far shore for another group. Holt and a dozen elves, all of them stripped to their breeches, had circled around the landing and reached the riverbank a half mile upstream from the ferry line. Syssal and the rest of his elves, unseen from Holt's vantage, closed in on the landing, trying to slip through the ring of watching trolls. Danis, much to her disgust, had been persuaded to remain behind on the bluff. After ten minutes of stubborn, angry argument, the Daryman had convinced her that, in the event things went terribly wrong, she must remain safe from capture if Vanderthan were to have a chance of victory.

With grim satisfaction Holt saw ranks of heavily armored footmen marching onto the raft, until once again the heavy craft was tightly packed with Erik's soldiers and wallowed low from the weight of metal and men. Some of the troops carried poles, but they started across by pulling on the rope— apparently they brought the wooden shafts in case of an emergency.

Holt resolved to give them just that.

As the ferry raft started back across the Tannyv, the Daryman and the elves with him slipped into the clear, flowing water. Goose bumps sprouted from Holt's skin as he was immediately reminded that, not too many miles away, this river began as melting snow. Forcing himself to dive, he shivered under the surface, stroking and kicking strongly as he pulled away from the bank.

The Lodestone Blade was secured tightly to Holt's waist, and impeded his legs only slightly. He accepted the interference as a necessary drawback, since the weapon was an important part of their plan. Carried by a surprisingly strong current, the swimmers sought to stay low, sticking their heads up just high enough to allow them to breathe.

Despite its placid appearance, the Tannyv bobbed and roiled with deceptive force. Holt wondered if they could remain unobserved, knowing there was nothing he could do about it in any event. Swiftly they floated downstream, the elves swimming powerfully toward the center of the river while Holt allowed himself to bob along halfway between the river center and the shore.

Shouts rose from the woods around the ferry landing, and Holt knew that Syssal Kipican's archers had struck. Even if the trolls could not be permanently harmed by the steel-tipped arrows, he hoped that the distraction would be enough to hold the attention of the troops on shore and aboard the ferry. Indeed, as he bobbed over a swell, he saw the men on the raft anxiously staring toward the landing. None seemed to pay attention to the water itself.

The Daryman was almost even with the ferry line now. Were the swimming elves in place? He couldn't worry—the current pushed him into the partially submerged rope with surprising force. Grasping the hefty line, which was as thick as his arm, Holt carefully drew the Lodestone Blade. The water slowed the force of his blows, but he struck and sawed at the rope, swiftly hewing through the many strands of hemp.

Abruptly the last of the line was sliced, and the current carried the Daryman through the sudden gap. He heard cries of alarm and, as the water swelled beneath him, saw the troops on the ferry jabbing their poles into the water, seeking to arrest the sudden downstream rush.

Those poles thrust into the water but then, one by one, the men grasping the shafts tumbled over the sides of the raft as the shafts were snatched away. The submerged elves attacked speedily, with complete surprise, swiftly removing the last means of controlling the ferry. In moments the raft swirled madly, completely out of control.

Swimming strongly now, Holt made for the foot of the bluff where Danis remained concealed. Shouts of panic rang out, and several crossbow bolts whizzed past Holt's head, but soon he had drifted out of range of the troops on the near shore—and those on the raft were too busy clinging for their lives to shoot.

His limbs were numb from the long immersion in icy water. The current increased as he was swept downstream from the sliced ferry line. The river narrowed, and the surface grew more tumultuous. The same forces that hopefully would destroy the ferry now threatened to carry the Daryman himself to a chilly doom.

Holt's arms grew leaden with fatigue. He could barely find the strength to kick his legs. Looking upward, he saw the crest of the high bluff, thought of Danis concealed there—no doubt anxiously watching his struggles.

Hope fueled his body as he found the strength to kick, to pull his cupped hands firmly through the rapids. A rock bruised his side, but he pushed away from the barrier and splashed through an eddy near the steep bank.

Then his feet touched bottom, and he wearily crawled onto the rocky shore. Mindful of the nearby trolls, he slipped into the shelter of a narrow ravine and made his way as quickly as possible upward. He rested, gasping for breath every dozen steps or so, but none of the horrid predators appeared before he reached the full cover of the higher forest.

"Holt! You made it! I was so scared!"

Danis met him at the edge of the cliff. Gratefully

he leaned on the princess, allowing her to help him to her hideout—a clearing behind several mossy oak trunks.

"The raft?" he asked weakly, looking back to the river.

"Gone—smashed in the rapids."

One by one the elven swimmers joined them until ten of the twelve sodden elves squatted with the two humans in the shelter. After a full hour had silently passed, they grimly accepted the fact that two of their comrades had been lost in the perilous mission.

Syssal Kipican joined them, accepting the news of his dead warriors with stiff formality. Still, Holt saw a tightening of the elven leader's shoulders and sensed that—underneath his steely facade— Syssal grieved terribly at the losses.

"Look—up the river," one of the elves muttered. "I think they have another raft."

With sinking spirits Holt stared at the cove on the far bank that was indicated by the elf's pointing finger. He saw another broad ferry, as large as the first, slowly drift into the current.

"They'll *still* get across!" the Daryman groaned, a sense of inevitable disaster sweeping over him.

"We could never stop them, you know," Syssal said, laying a calming hand on Holt's shoulder.

"They must have been planning to use both of them," Danis said. "This way, it will take them twice as long to cross."

"We've bought ourselves a day or two," Holt agreed, thinking about the teeming horde that would soon gather in Greenbriar. "We can only hope that it's enough."

21
Scourge of Greenbriar

As the new raft approached, Holt saw numerous
bowmen encircling the craft's perimeter. They held
their weapons high, ready to shoot at anything in
the water. As the ferry drew nearer the bank, he
saw that, furthermore, Rockeford's army now used
two ropes instead of one for their ferry line. Any
further attempt to sabotage the operation in the
water would clearly be doomed to failure.

By nightfall five more crossings had been made,
and many hundreds of human warriors joined the
trolls in the sanctified ground of the Greenbriar

Forest. Syssal gritted his teeth and cursed in real pain as Erik's troops felled trees and built numerous, massive bonfires. Soon the uninterrupted forest was defiled by a barren, muddy clearing along the riverbank, where the Army of Rockeford and its troll allies made themselves a camp.

That night a larger company of elven archers joined the companions on the hilltop. These silent, serious warriors numbered over a hundred, and each of them carried a quiver full of sleek, steel-headed arrows. But already they were outnumbered five to one by the invaders. From the height of their bluff they were too far away for effective shooting, and the vigilance of the trolls made any closer approach too dangerous except for brief, skirmishing raids, so the elven warriors could only join the others in agonizing frustration.

"We should start back to Vanderthan with the dawn," Holt urged the princess as sunset brought their observations—and the enemy's river crossing operation—to a close.

"No! It's important that we stay here, keep our eyes on Sir Erik! Sir Ira has carried word to father, and we can't do any more than that."

The Daryman was about to press the argument, but something in her look stopped him. Instead, he settled in for another night of restless waiting.

For two more days the raft plied its course across the river, bringing chariots, horses, additional trolls, and many, many companies of the black-garbed infantry. How many thousands of warriors were poised to march toward the city Holt couldn't tell, but it seemed that—even without the Crown of Vanderthan—Sir Erik's army would have no difficulty overwhelming King Dathwell's forces.

"Where's Gallarath?" Danis demanded as the sun set on the last day of the crossing.

"Four days was his best estimate," Holt remembered—knowing full well that Danis had been involved in the same conversation. "He may have encountered difficulties."

"Or it could be that he is marching to the edge of the forest, downstream from here. That would be the logical place to make a stand against them," Syssal suggested.

"You're right," the Daryman agreed. "The whole army's across now—I would expect them to resume the march with the sunrise."

"What about you and your archers?" Danis asked the elven captain, fixing him with a stern look. "If this army marches out of the forest, are you going to let them go?"

"The desecration of Greenbriar cannot pass unchallenged," Syssal replied bluntly. "When they cut down the first tree, they brought the elves into this campaign against them. We lack the numbers to make a stand, but know that they will feel the sting of our arrows as they move through the wood. And if it proves that your human allies can muster in time for battle, we will fight at your sides."

"That's as much—perhaps *more*—than I could ask," the princess said, her tone softening. She looked around in surprise, realizing that once again the three of them were alone on the bluff. "Where did your warriors go?"

"They already take up positions near the enemy camp. We've observed that the trolls gather in the camp—perhaps to eat, or else to listen to the commands of their lord. In any event, elven eyes are keen in the dark—the invaders will not sleep well tonight."

No sooner had Syssal spoken than a commotion rose from Sir Erik's army. Men rushed to the near end of the camp, pointing to the woods and gesturing to a trio of men who lay still on the ground. Even in the dim light, the companions could see the silvery arrows jutting from the victims.

Immediately a figure in black armor strode forward, gesturing to the woods. Hundreds of men and trolls rushed toward the trees, shouting and brandishing their swords.

"Your elves!" cried Danis in alarm.

"They've already withdrawn," Syssal replied confidently. "No human or troll can catch an elven scout in the forest of Greenbriar." His shook his head regretfully. "Alas, such tactics will only annoy them. My small force can be little more than a nuisance."

"If it helps to slow Erik long enough for Dathwell and Gallarath to arrive, that will be a great service," the princess replied. She gestured to the figure in black, who was barely a spot of darkness at this distance, and spoke in a voice heavy with loathing. "That must be the Grand Knight of Rockeford."

"Would that I could score a hit from a mile away," Syssal said grimly. "That would solve a multitude of our problems."

"Perhaps," Holt said. "But I've seen his armor, and I doubt that an arrow could penetrate it. And even if he fell, the forces of Entropy would still hold the crown. *That's* the greatest threat."

The long, dark night passed slowly. Often screams of pain or outrage exploded from Erik's army, proving that the elven archers remained effective at their nocturnal work. Yet when dawn revealed the camp teeming with activity, Holt knew that Syssal's estimate was true. The elves could merely harass the army. They would never be able to stop it.

They watched in silence as columns of troops formed up and horses were hitched to chariots or saddled. The trolls, hissing and barking, entered the woods—presumably to drive the elven warriors back to a safe distance.

"They're getting ready to march," Danis observed.

"*Now* we should move down the riverbank," Holt suggested. "There's nothing more we can do here—and we have to stay in front of their march. At least that way we can give some information to Prince Gallarath or King Dathwell."

Throughout the day the two humans on horseback, with Syssal trotting on foot and acting as guide, hastened through the wood. Frequently elven scouts appeared, reporting to their chieftain on the progress of the enemy's advance. "The chariots are having some trouble in the woods," one of these warriors informed them. "That seems to be slowing the whole army down considerably."

By nightfall the companions were several miles in front of the lumbering formation, but even so Holt and Danis pressed ahead until full darkness prevented any further progress. They made a small camp in the shelter of a huge oak. The Daryman built a fire while the princess sat on a log and glumly stared into the shadows.

"I say," came a familiar voice from the branches above. "*There* you are!"

"Sir Ira!" cried Danis, leaping to her feet. "What's the word from my father?"

"King Dathwell and such men as he could muster will meet you at the edge of the wood, less than a day's march downstream from here."

"That's wonderful!"

"Er, perhaps. However, he has but a few small companies of footmen, and one rank of cavalry. I fear that Sir Erik's army has him terribly overmatched."

Huddled around their small blaze, Holt, Danis,

and Syssal described for Sir Ira the steady advance of the enemy force. Blinking his yellow eyes in alarm, the owl nodded sagely.

When they had completed the tale, he spoke. "I should fly ahead and inform the king. At the very least he can pick a place to make his stand—and we can hope that the prince is as good as his word."

"But at night? Shouldn't you wait until dawn?" the princess asked.

"Posh and downfeathers! I'm quite capable of winging through the woods in the dark!" Sir Ira huffed. In a swoop of widespread wings, he disappeared.

The companions started out at first light, pressing through the woods with renewed haste. By midmorning they reached the fringe of the great wood, advancing into a riverside plain of pasture and meadow. On a distant hilltop fluttered the banners of Vanderthan, and the two humans and the elf hastened toward King Dathwell's force.

As they climbed the gentle slope Holt looked in vain for some sign of Prince Gallarath. The ground rose gradually away from the river and he could see for many miles. But though his eyes beheld a pastoral vista of trees, pastures, and lanes, he found nothing hopeful in that scene.

"My darling! You're safe!" hailed the king as the companions rode up to his encampment. Behind the hill they saw tents and corrals, where men-at-arms polished weapons or huddled around cook-fires. After the mass of Rockeford's army, this seemed to be a pathetically small force.

"Tut, tut—you gave us all a scare, my dear," Tellist Tizzit declared, blinking back an unusual moisture in his eyes.

"Oh, Father—and Tellist! This is all my fault!" cried Danis, leaping from her saddle and sobbing into the king's arms.

"Now, I'm certain that scoundrel would have set out on this plot with or without the crown," Dathwell comforted. "If anyone's to blame, it's me—I wish I'd never thought of this wretched contest! To think, I invited him to my castle, fed him at my table—and sent him questing with my daughter!"

"*I* went questing on my own, remember?" Danis sniffed, squeezing the distraught king's shoulders.

"Holton! You're safe!"

The Daryman looked up in surprise and elation as Derek Jaken called to him from the back of a hay-stacked cart. Holt saw that his father had ridden in relative comfort with King Dathwell's marching troops.

"Sir Ira tells us there's trolls comin' along with Sir Erik," the elder Daryman explained. "Thought I might be able to offer some advice on fighting the buggers, since it wasn't that long ago I was doin' it myself."

Holt thought of his deductions regarding the Grand Knight of Rockeford. "Not only trolls, but

trolls under the same commander as before," he said grimly. He recounted the description of the man's mangled hand, and the artificial fingers in the glove.

"That's him!" Derek declared, his face washing to a bloodless hue. "By the spheres—and I never suspected it when I saw him! He's changed a lot, and not just from age. He's a bigger man, now, and it seems he's learned to mask his cruelty—at least, for a time. But why didn't I know?"

"It couldn't be helped," King Dathwell consoled. "His change of appearance was fairly complete. Certainly he would never have dared to enter Vanderthan if he thought there was a chance he'd be recognized. Besides, enough talk of what has gone before. Come, I need all of your counsels for what is yet to come."

The weary travelers retired to the royal pavilion, and there bathed and ate and dressed their wounds. The meal was joyous despite the grave battle that lay ahead. Men cheered, and more banners flew to welcome the princess, but as the Daryman looked around his heart sank. The men of Vanderthan were true and brave, he knew, but compared to the size of Sir Erik's force they were little more than a hastily assembled band. Even with the addition of Syssal's elves, who trooped out of the woods later in the day, the entire defensive force remained terribly outnumbered.

By late afternoon the first trolls appeared at the

edge of the forest. The slick, green-skinned monsters advanced a little way into a wide pasture, and then stopped. The companions watched in dismay as more and more of Erik's troops emerged, forming companies across the wide fields, preparing camps for the night.

"They'll attack in the morning," Syssal guessed, as he joined Holt, the king, Derek, and the princess at the hilltop observation post."

"Where is Gallarath?" demanded Danis. "He said it might take him four days—he's two days overdue!"

"And what about these trolls?" the king asked. "They heal themselves even after they're killed, you know! Seems a bit of a sticky problem."

"We have to burn 'em," Derek replied in confirmation. "Tell the men to concentrate several swords against a single troll. Then, when the thing falls, a detail of men has to be ready to pour oil over the body and touch a torch to it. If we do that, and do it quick enough, we'll be able to kill—I mean, *really* kill—the brutes."

"Splendid. Good plan." The king turned to his daughter. "Derek insisted that we bring every cask of oil in the city, so we should be set for it. I'll go assign the men to the burning details."

Holt had been squinting, staring along the crest of the inland ridge.

"What's that?" he asked, pointing. Something moved there, far away—a long file marching down a track between two hills. Evening sunlight glimmered from silvery speartips.

Gallarath was on the way!

Sir Ira winged outward to guide the prince of Rochester to the hilltop position. Though the first elements of the reinforcements didn't arrive until nearly midnight, a jolt of optimism spread quickly through the Vanderthan forces—especially when they saw that Gallarath's force was at least twice as big as Dathwell's and the elves combined.

The prince himself, accompanied by a dashing youngster who could not quite grow a full beard—though not for lack of trying—rode into the camp with the lead columns. The prince of Rochester dismounted and bowed low to Danis. "My princess!" he declared. "I come with my legion, sworn to fight in your name!"

"I'm glad to see you," Danis replied, stepping forward to embrace the prince. Even through his elation Holt felt a stab of familiar resentment. What could a farmboy, even armed with the Lodestone Blade, offer to compete with this nobleman?

"This is my brother, Wallas." The prince introduced his youthful companion. "He's come to get a taste of war."

"Welcome," the princess said. "Though I wish we could greet you under different circumstances."

"What could be more exciting?" Wallas asked, grinning as he slipped from his saddle and bounced lightly to the ground. "When do we attack?"

"Attack?" Holt asked in disbelief. "Even with the addition of your forces, we're still outnumbered. At least we have this hilltop—if we wait for Sir Erik to come to us, we can meet him with the advantage of height."

"Wait?" Prince Gallarath cocked an arrogant eyebrow. "Young man, in war the initiative is everything! Erik will certainly be expecting us to wait for him. Therefore, we must do what he does not expect—and that is to attack."

"Er, doesn't that seem just a trifle rash?" asked King Dathwell. "I understand the importance of surprise—but elevation has an advantage of its own. If we sacrifice that—"

"Sacrifice? Your Majesty, of course not. After all, when we attack, we'll charge *down* the hill. That will give added impetus to our charge—with enough force to smash these rascals and send them fleeing from the field!"

"But if we fail—?" Danis, like her father, sounded unconvinced.

Prince Gallarath stood to his full height. His eyes flashed as he glared at the king, the princess, Syssal Kipican, and Holton Jaken. "The Army of Rochester will charge at dawn," he declared. "You are welcome to join in my assault. If not, I shall be forced to carry the day without assistance."

Holt flushed. His fists clenched involuntarily, and he wanted to seize the prince by the shoulders and shake some sense of cooperation into him.

Even as he forced back the almost overwhelming urge, King Dathwell sighed.

"There may be some truth to what you say—certainly Erik won't expect an attack. In any event, if we divide our small force we face certain disaster. So, my good prince, the men of Vanderthan will advance at your side."

"As will the elves of Greenbriar," Syssal said tightly.

"Splendid!" cried Wallas, clapping his elder brother on the shoulder. "Now, shouldn't we have a feast or something?"

"*After* the battle," Danis said grimly.

"For those of us who are left," Holt added, muttering under his breath. Gallarath looked at him sharply, but made no reply.

"We attack at dawn, then," King Dathwell agreed, slumping in resignation. "Perhaps, for now, we had better get some rest. I have a feeling that tomorrow's going to be a long day."

22
Battle of Tannyvheight

The men of Rochester and Vanderthan, together with the elves of Greenbriar, silently moved into position for the attack. The predawn mists swirled around them, obscuring vision beyond a few feet. Holt led Old Thunder toward the center of the line, where Danis and Prince Gallarath also gathered. Here, too, were the small numbers of Vanderthan and Rochester's horsemen. The men on foot would charge in long ranks to the right and left.

The Daryman realized, in a moment of stark apprehension, that he missed Fenrald Falwhak—

terribly! The dwarf's steady competence would have been a great comfort to Holt as butterflies of nervous energy fluttered through his stomach. He felt for a moment as though he were going to be sick. Then Danis appeared in the darkness, and he bit back the bile, determined to put on a brave front.

Prince Gallarath, on the other hand, seemed to project courage and calm without even trying. The Son of Rochester rode his horse at an easy walk, swinging lightly to the ground when he met the princess.

"My companies are formed in line abreast," he said. "They'll charge when I give the order."

"The men of Vanderthan will do the same," Danis replied. "I just came from my father. He and Tellist are in the center of the line—they'll lead the charge." She shivered when she spoke, and Holt knew that her tremors were not caused by the morning chill.

"Syssal's elves marched nearly two hours ago," Holt confirmed. "He should be in position by now."

"Good." Gallarath looked at the sky, where misty clouds already dissipated to reveal a pale blue expanse. "They should have no difficulty seeing the first rays of dawn." They had agreed the previous night that sunlight striking the tallest tree on the hilltop would be the signal to initiate the attack.

Night's shadows withdrew to reveal the river

and the field below. Breakfast fires smoldered in the midst of Erik's army, and sentries paced along the perimeter of the vast camp. Most of the troops of Rockeford, however, had just begun to stir.

On the hilltop, the men of the troll-burning details, supervised by the younger prince of Rochester, trundled casks of oil from the carts, each man filling several skins with the flammable liquid.

"Are the torches ready?" the princess asked Gallarath.

"Aye. Wallas was none too happy about a rearguard task, but when I told him about the trolls he seemed to understand."

"I hope so," Holt noted grimly. "If we don't have men ready to burn their corpses after we chop them up, they'll heal so fast that they'll be attacking us from behind."

"He'll do as he was told," the prince barked. His eyes flashed upward, where the first rays of the sun cast a halo across the high treetops. "We'd best be ready to attack."

As he spoke they heard cries of alarm from the men in Sir Erik's army. Silvery shafts sparkled in the sun, arcing outward from a clump of trees on the far side of the invading force. Volleys of elven arrows fell first on the sentries, and then amid the men who scrambled to meet the threat.

"That's Syssal," Holt said.

The elves of Greenbriar were trying to make the enemy fear that the attack was coming from the opposite side of the camp. From the initial confusion, it looked like the tactic had succeeded.

"Let's go!" cried Gallarath.

Old Thunder pawed the ground, and as Holt drew the Lodestone Blade, he found that his hands trembled with excitement. Footmen surged forward while Danis—astride the prancing Lancer—drew her own blade and pulled into the lead. The Daryman pressed his big horse after, determined not to let the young woman out of his sight.

Now confusion reigned in Sir Erik's camp, as the attackers came into view on the wide hillside. Men of Vanderthan and Rochester raised their voices in lusty battle cries, and not until his throat was raw did Holt realize that he was adding to the din. To his right, over the heads of a rank of swordsmen, he saw the pennant of King Dathwell, and he recognized the whiskered form of Tellist Tizzit riding beside the monarch.

To the other side, the men of Rochester swept ahead. Gallarath was the picture of warlike fury—his blond hair swept back by the wind, his axe upraised before him. The prince howled like a wolf, a cry that was echoed by many of the men behind him.

The ground swept past, and in moments Old Thunder carried Holt into the guards at the edge of the enemy camp. Swordsmen tried to form a line of defense, but the attackers knocked them aside without delay. The Daryman was vaguely aware of men going down beneath his horse's massive hooves, but only after they breached the first line did Holt realize that, somehow, his sword had gotten blood on it.

Thundering hooves echoed through the camp as armored horsemen raced to the counterattack. Holt slashed at a lancer's long-shafted weapon, chopping it in two. When the rider drew his sword the Daryman bashed the blade out of the way and cut the man from his saddle.

All around horses bucked and reared. Danis cried out in pain when a heavy knight smashed a mace against her shoulder. The princess swayed in her saddle as Old Thunder lunged, giving Holt a clear swing at the knight. Quickly the Lodestone Blade cut through the fellow's iron shoulder plate, inflicting a painful wound.

Someone clutched at Holt's leg and he looked down to see a dismounted knight trying to drag him from the saddle. Once again the gray-bladed sword slashed, and another of the invaders went down, groaning. Old Thunder reared, pulling momentarily above the melee, and the Daryman saw that their charge had carried them far into Sir Erik's camp. Desperately he looked around, seeking some sign of the treacherous knight—or the crown he had stolen. Though countless men raced toward the attackers, Holt saw nothing of the deceitful suitor.

"Onward!" shouted Gallarath, pushing free of

the defending lancers. Holt and Danis raced beside him while many of the Rochester footmen circled around the horsemen of Rockeford.

They rode among many still forms, and Holt saw silvery arrows jutting from these. Syssal Kipican's archers had done deadly work, and as he looked ahead the Daryman saw the elves break from their wooded copses, advancing with shining swords drawn against the rear of the army camp.

"Forward! For Rochester and Vanderthan!" howled Gallarath, his voice shrill with battle-fury. Holt found himself echoing the cry, stunned—and frightened—by his own elation. He saw the ranks of the attackers pressing through the surprised, disorganized defenders, and for the first time since the battle began, he dared to hope that the prince's mad plan had a chance of success.

More footmen scrambled to meet the charge, but now it seemed that the advance built unstoppable momentum. Holt hacked and chopped, watching in surprise as the men of Rockeford turned and fled even before his blade could fall. All around, Erik's shocked troops recoiled, falling steadily back at first, but soon turning in outright panic, fleeing from the onslaught.

Larger forms loomed beyond the routing humans. Erik's men cried out in horror and turned from their own allies as packs of trolls charged toward the fight. The grotesque monsters seized the fleeing men and cast them out of the way, often inflicting worse wounds than those done by the swords of Vanderthan and Rochester.

A hulking troll lunged at the Daryman, and again Holt shivered at the sight of those black, empty eyes—the orbs of Entropy. Snarling from the force of his fury, the Daryman chopped with his keen blade, dropping the monster with a single powerful blow.

"Fire! Bring up the fire!" cried Gallarath, turning to face a trio of the green-skinned monsters. The beasts clawed at the prince's horse while the nobleman slashed back and forth, striving to hold the creatures at bay.

A ball of flaming, oily heat suddenly sizzled in the midst of the trolls, expanding into a searing cloud, roiling upward with black smoke and the putrid stench of burned trolls. Instinctively, Holt knew that this was the work of Tellist Tizzit—and, remembering some accidental effects of the wizard's previous spells, the Daryman thanked the spheres that the deadly fireball had fallen on the enemy.

Next a bolt of lightning crackled through the monsters, sending them barking and scrambling away from the magic-user.

Gallarath groaned, and Holt's attention whirled back. The Daryman saw the prince of Rochester dragged from his saddle by a massive, snarling troll. The monster raised its bloodstained talons in a victorious gesture of triumph, while the man twisted helplessly in its grip. Other trolls dragged Gallarath's unfortunate horse to the ground, where it whinnied in shrill terror until the monsters ended its miseries.

Desperately Holt jabbed his heels into Old Thunder's flanks. The horse surged forward, pressing aside a pair of howling trolls—one of which shied away from the Lodestone Blade. The other didn't see the weapon's slicing blow until it was too late. Just as the huge troll seized Gallarath's throat, Holt reached the melee, leaning forward and cutting the brute down with a hard, chopping slash.

"Thanks, my good man!" the prince declared heartily, springing to his feet.

"Here—up behind me!" shouted Holt, extending a hand. In another moment Gallarath sprang onto Thunder's hindquarters, staying mounted with the pressure of his knees while he held axe and shield in his hands.

Together the two humans clung to the big horse as Old Thunder pitched and bucked in the midst of the trolls. One of the monsters lunged at the reins, and Holt cut it down. Two more charged toward the tail—the prince's axe carved a deep wound in one of these while Thunder's heavy rear hooves smashed the other to the ground.

In short order three more trolls joined their fellows on the ground, and the others quickly saw that the wounds—at least those from the Lode-

stone Blade—did not heal. The grotesque creatures fell back, and Holt took advantage of their
fear to lunge this way and that. Old Thunder
snorted like a war stallion, pounding toward one
band of trolls after another, and with each rush the
morale of the horrific creatures faded.

Some of them scrambled backward, falling to
the ground in panic or barking in fear as they
jumped away. With each of Holt's attacks the monsters' fear grew, until a dozen turned and fled
when Old Thunder snorted in their direction.

"After them! The battle is won!" cried Gallarath
in elation.

Holt, too, felt a flush of victory. A look over his
shoulder showed that Wallas's men were dousing
the felled trolls with oil and torching them, insuring that even those dropped by mundane weapons
would stay slain. Meanwhile, Danis rallied a band
of Vanderthan's men, and behind her, King Dathwell and Tellist Tizzit charged forward against a
fresh company of Sir Erik's defenders.

Abruptly a company of men in the lead of the
attack ceased their advance, halting to collapse on
the ground in exhaustion. They looked as though,
as a group, they had decided to stop fighting and
lie down for a nap!

"Up! Up, you fools!" cried Dathwell, urging his
horse among them. Suddenly the king dismounted
and lay down among his men, resting his hands
over his ample belly as his chest rose up and down

from the rhythm of his snores.

Only then did Holt see the figure beyond, riding a black horse along the front of battle. Sir Erik's black armor gleamed, and the sword in his hands was crimson with blood. His charger's nostrils snorted, and cold, utterly arrogant contempt masked the knight's dark eyes. The Daryman saw all of these details, and one more—a sight that made everything else unimportant.

On his head, Sir Erik of Rockeford wore the Crown of Vanderthan. The silver circlet glowed with a light of its own, and everywhere around the treacherous knight, Erik's enemies ceased fighting.

Horrified, Holt saw Sir Erik bark a command at a group of Vanderthan's swordsmen. The men immediately dropped their weapons and began to kick up their heels in a frantic dance. The knight's face curled into an aloof, almost bored sneer.

Then Erik turned to Tellist Tizzit. The wizard was only a couple of paces away when the knight gave another order.

The Daryman saw Tellist making the distinct hand gestures of a spell, and knew that the magic user was working some enchantment. Yet when he finished, the wizard clapped his hands against *himself!* Immediately he rose from the ground, kicking and flailing, floating rapidly upward into the sky.

"Over there—let me strike the rogue from his

saddle!" Gallarath commanded from the back of Old Thunder.

"We can't!" the Daryman objected miserably. "Can't you see what he's doing? He wears the Crown of Vanderthan! If we get close to him, he'll simply order us to take a nap, or dance—or worse! And we won't have any choice but to obey!"

"Maybe *you'll* have no choice," declared the prince. "But no knight tells the prince of Rochester what to do!"

Before Holt could object Gallarath slipped off the back of Old Thunder. The prince seized the reins of a passing, riderless horse, and quickly swung into the saddle.

"Wait!" cried Holt—and Danis, as well, who rode close in time to see what the nobleman intended.

Along the front, more of Vanderthan's men ceased to fight. Some of them started to bicker with their comrades, while others squatted and used their blades to trim their fingernails or shave.

Gallarath reined in before Sir Erik. Mutely the prince of Rochester dismounted, kneeling in the mud before the knight's horse. As Erik chuckled in wry amusement, the nobleman repeated the humiliating gesture again and again.

"What can we do?" Danis asked miserably, edging closer to the knight.

"I don't know," Holt replied, equally despairing. "Stay back—it looks like the crown's powers of command work up to only twenty or thirty feet away from Erik."

"Syssal's archers!" Danis said. "Maybe—"

Holt, too, had thought of this possibility. Now he looked, however, and saw that the trolls had regrouped and driven the elves back in a furious rush. The men of Rochester, dismayed by their prince's irrational behavior, had also begun to fall back.

In a few moments the entire army, or what was left of it, collapsed around the Daryman and the princess. They had no choice but to fall back with their warriors, back toward the long and muddy slope of the hill. Behind them they left the king, the prince, and fully half of their numbers in the thrall of Sir Erik and the artifact of the immortals.

23
Fight For the Crown

Holton looked across the battlefield and saw nothing but disaster. The scope of catastrophe dragged him down, made him want to weep in despair, but some reserve of martial spirit kept him retreating toward the crest of the hill, calling as many warriors as he could to rally around the banners of Vanderthan and Rochester.

Some men answered that call, but many others looked at the spectacle wrought by Sir Erik and the Crown of Vanderthan: King Dathwell napped comfortably while Prince Gallarath still knelt in the mud, offering fealty to the dark knight who had already ridden away. Tellist continued to rise into the air, levitating so quickly that Holt could barely spot him—a dark speck against the incongruously sunny sky. The wind had begun to carry the wizard downstream along the course of the river.

Looking at the battlefield, Holt realized with despair that the effects of the crown's commands lasted long after the wearer rode out of range of those he had compelled to obey. The Daryman could only hope that if Sir Erik could be killed—or the crown somehow removed from his head—the effect would be broken. And he didn't see how even that slim hope could be tested.

Across the field many mounds of troll bodies smoldered, spewing oily black smoke into the air. Yet still more of the horrific humanoids survived, and now these monsters gathered around Sir Erik of Rockeford.

Erik's human warriors, too, had begun to reform their companies—though hundreds had been slain in the initial attack. Still, those who remained easily outnumbered the men that the Daryman and Danis Vanderthan tried to gather on the hilltop. Even without the trolls, the final stand of the battle could have but one outcome. The addition of the monstrous troops simply made the end more horrifying.

"The attack was faring well—for a while," observed an armored human warrior on the ground beside Old Thunder. Holt looked down as the man removed a bracelet from his wrist.

"Syssal!" cried the Daryman, feeling a momentary flicker of joy. "I see that you have survived—so far."

"Aye—though too many of my countrymen will never again walk the trails of Greenbriar," declared the elf bitterly.

"Your arrows gave us the chance for great headway," Danis said, riding Lancer to Holt's side. "But nothing is sufficient to hold against the crown!" She shook her head bitterly. "If only I hadn't—"

"Stop it!" Holt demanded, and Danis surprised him by obeying. "What can we do right now?"

"We can stand only so long as Sir Erik is elsewhere," Syssal observed, pointing down the slope. "The trolls hold my archers back—and those who have gotten close enough to shoot have found that the man's armor is simply too thick. We can't hurt him with arrows."

At the foot of the hill a small knot of Gallarath's men formed a square of bristling spears, holding a press of swordsmen at bay. Sir Erik galloped past the square, shouting commands that were inaudible above the roar of the battle.

His words became clear enough as soon as he passed, when the men of Rochester threw down their weapons and embraced each other, cavorting like madmen over the bodies strewn across the ground. Danis groaned in despair as the attackers rushed into the breached square, quickly surrounding the men who remained in control of their own will. Those who did not surrender were quickly and mercilessly slaughtered.

Another group of men wearing the blue and gold of Vanderthan formed a line against the pursuit. These troops bore swords and carried heavy shields. They stood shoulder to shoulder and, for a few moments, beat back the press of Rockeford attackers. Yet even before he could feel a flash of hope Holt saw Sir Erik turn toward that island of resistance. In a few moments, the Crown of Vanderthan's powers once again thwarted the courage of loyal men.

A blare of trumpets sounded across the field, the brash sound rising over the din with a clarion cry. The pace of the fighting slowed momentarily, as men from both sides looked about for the source of the sound.

"What's that?" Holt asked, turning to where Syssal had been standing. There was no sign of the elf, though several warriors hurried down the hill, returning to the fight. On one of them the Daryman saw a flash of silver glinting at the wrist.

"Look!" cried Danis, tautly hopeful. She pointed along the bank of the Tannyv, upstream beyond Sir Erik's camp.

Again those trumpets brayed, and now Holt saw movement in the distance. A file of warriors clumped forward at a trot, and when the horns rang out again he saw the glint of sun off brass. The newcomers were signaling their arrival.

"Who are they?" the princess asked, frightened. Holt knew her fear: could these be more troops of Rockeford, coming to aid their black knight when he stood on the verge of victory?

Squinting, the Daryman didn't think so. The phalanx of armored warriors came on, expanding into a broader column as they neared the fight. Even in the distance, Holt detected something familiar about the newcomers' rolling gait, their stocky posture.

"Dwarves!" he cried, suddenly certain. "It's Fenrald Falwhak and the dwarves of Graywall!"

They watched in disbelief as the dwarven column smashed through the camp of Sir Erik's army, driving the knight's troops back wherever they clashed. Trolls swarmed toward the dwarves and went down beneath a curtain of slashing steel—swords, hammers, and axes swirled rapidly, bashing the monsters to earth. As the dwarves passed over the grotesque corpses, some of them stopped to douse the mangled trolls with oil, or touch torches to the sodden remains. Soon many more columns of black smoke marked the places where trolls had fallen.

"Come on!" cried Holt, seizing the crumb of hope. The dwarven attack disrupted Sir Erik's pursuit as the companies of Rockeford turned to face this threat to the rear. "Down the hill!" shouted the

Daryman, urging Old Thunder into a lumbering gallop.

Astride fleet Lancer, Danis rode beside him, adding her own voice to the din.

The surviving warriors of Vanderthan and Rochester, seeing the example of the princess and the Daryman, roared their own approval and surged down the hill once more in a wave of flesh and steel. Prince Wallas and his men had avoided the effects of the crown, and now they charged with torches and oil, bringing up the rear of the advancing force.

Again Holt felt the exhilarating rush of the charge, the sweeping momentum carrying him along in a battle haze. Yet this time, in the back of his mind, he knew that the stakes were beyond desperate. If they didn't shatter Erik's army, they would die in the attempt—and still they had no way to deal with the Crown of Vanderthan's powers!

Old Thunder trampled a troll, and the Daryman slashed his sword, driving another of the monsters out of Danis's path. The princess on her charger swept past, her steel blade chopping to the right and left in lightning strokes.

A flash of silver gleamed over the shoulders of the trolls, and the brutes parted to reveal Sir Erik. The crown on his head glowed with an unnatural light—but now his eyes, too, had taken on a bizarre gleam.

"Look out!" Holt cried as Danis continued her charge. Only with his warning did she twist her head to see the knight galloping toward her.

The princess pulled hard on Lancer's reins, spinning the black horse to the side. Powerful rear hooves kicked up bits of sod as Lancer lunged away from Sir Erik. Danis dropped low in the saddle, clinging to the reins.

One of the trolls leapt with the speed of a striking snake, slashing at Lancer's head. The horse twisted away, and those awful talon's hooked into Danis's shoulder. With a cry of pain, she flew from the saddle and smashed heavily to the ground.

Old Thunder reared as Holt jerked the big horse to a halt. Trolls swarmed close, and he struck two down with quick blows. The others quickly fell back. But beyond the monsters, twenty or thirty paces away, he saw Sir Erik sitting astride his horse. The knight approached with an expression of cool detachment, looking down at the groaning form of the princess of Vanderthan.

"Rise, wench," he ordered. "Clean off some of that mud before you present yourself to the conqueror of Vanderthan!"

Appalled, Holt watched Danis climb to her feet. Her movements were slow, awkward, as if someone tugged at her limbs with invisible force. With a sickening certainty, he knew what was happening—the Crown of Vanderthan's power compelled her to obey Sir Erik's commands!

The Daryman urged his big horse forward, and Sir Erik cast him a quick glance. "Dismount, farm-boy—and perform a dance for me!"

Holt jerked back on the reins, furious. He remained some distance away from the knight and felt no compulsion to obey the command. Still, he knew that if he rode any closer he, as surely as Dathwell, Gallarath, Tellist, and the princess, would be forced to obey Sir Erik's wishes.

The knight sneered before he dropped his gaze back to the princess. Swinging his leg easily from his stirrup, Sir Erik sprang to the ground, leaving the reins of his horse with a warrior who had stepped forward to take them. Swaggering, the knight advanced toward the princess.

"Kneel, woman—kneel before your new king!"

Danis's head jolted backward as if she had been slapped. Her back rigid, she stood stiffly before the glowering knight.

"On your knees, wench! Do you hear?"

Somehow Danis found the strength to resist the command. Her legs trembled visibly, but she stood erect in the face of Erik's demands. Furiously, the knight took a step forward, raising his hand for a slap.

The Daryman groaned in frustration, drawing a look from the traitorous suitor—a look sufficient to keep Holt from advancing, though he dismounted and held the Lodestone Blade ready in his hand, desperate for any opportunity.

The man holding Sir Erik's charger dropped the reins and stepped after his leader. Holt wondered if the knight desired some kind of help. What was he going to do to Danis? At the same time, the Daryman saw something odd in the attendant's manner—he was not looking to *help* Erik of Rockeford.

The man's arm lashed out like a whip, but not so quickly that Holt couldn't see the silver bracelet there.

Syssal Kipican! The elf, disguised as a warrior of Rockeford, lunged at the crown.

Sensing the menace even before the elf's attack, Sir Erik whirled, bringing up his blade. Syssal's long fingers struck a point of the silver circlet as the knight stabbed. With a groan, Syssal slumped backward, bleeding from a deep wound in his chest.

Only then did Holt see that the Crown of Vanderthan no longer rested on Sir Erik's head. Instead, the elf had knocked it loose, sending it tumbling into the mud. Immediately Holt charged, raising the Lodestone Blade.

With a snarl of pure, animal rage, Sir Erik turned back to the princess. Danis, freed from the crown's thrall, tumbled backward, twisting on the ground, seeking the artifact of the immortals. The Daryman's heart broke—could he make it in time? He *had* to—or else his life would have no meaning.

Sir Erik drove his gore-streaked blade toward Danis's back as she fell to the muddy field and crawled away from him. Every muscle in Holt's body strained—wind whipped past his ears as he dived. His gray blade smashed the knight's weapon aside. Sir Erik's fury was redirected to the Daryman, and the villainous warrior lifted his sword for another smash.

On one knee, Holt parried the blow, smashing forcefully upward. The knight staggered back and the Daryman stood. Sir Erik's sword slashed, and again the Lodestone Blade knocked away the attack, but now Holt was forced to give ground.

The two weapons whirled against each other, the knight's skill countering the Lodestone Blade's power coupled with the basic techniques Holt had picked up from Fenrald's lessons over the summer. Frantically the Daryman twisted the sword back and forth, trying to anticipate each of the knight's lightning attacks. The weapon in Holt's hand seemed to have a mind, or at least instincts, of its own—the only way he could match his opponent was to forcibly relax and follow the lead of the enchanted blade.

Abruptly Sir Erik feinted an attack from the right, then came back with a vicious slash from the same side. Off-balance, Holt desperately parried the attack, feeling the hilt of his sword slide from his slippery palm. Desperately he squeezed his hand, pushing the blade forward as the knight stepped in for the kill.

The tip of the Lodestone Blade cut through Sir

Erik's armor as though it were a deerhide shield. The gray blade stabbed the Grand Knight of Rockeford in the chest, driving into his dark and murderous heart.

For a split second Sir Erik stood still, gazing stupidly at the ruins of his army and his life. Then he toppled, lying still with his face buried in the mud.

"Holt!" sobbed Danis, throwing her arms around his neck. Scarcely daring to breath, he sheathed his weapon and awkwardly returned her embrace.

He vaguely sensed the troops of Vanderthan gathering around, freed from the crown's potent compulsion. Beyond, the stunned troops of Rockeford fell back, appalled by the loss of their leader. King Dathwell ordered his men to let the routed troops go, knowing they would not be a threat to Vanderthan for the rest of their lives.

"Syssal," Holt said after a moment. They knelt beside their ally, sickened with worry at the pallor of his skin, the dullness of his eyes. Yet the slow rise and fall of his chest proved that he still lived.

"I say—looks as though I got here in the nick of time," declared Sir Ira, coming to light on the ground.

"Can you help him? He's badly hurt!" Danis pleaded.

"To what 'nick of time' do you think I was referring?" sniffed the owl. "Of course I can help. Now stand back, all of you."

"Danis! My daughter!" King Dathwell swept the princess into a bear hug. The monarch's tears fell unnoticed across his flushed cheeks.

"That was well done, my friend," Prince Gallarath said, warmly clapping Holt on the back. Even as the Daryman felt a surprising flush of pride, he saw that the prince's eyes lingered on the face of Danis Vanderthan.

"What's all this about holding a battle and not inviting the dwarves of Graywall?" huffed another voice as a stocky, battle-nicked warrior swaggered up the hill.

"Fenrald! You and your dwarves really saved the day," Holt declared, embracing the bewhiskered warrior.

"We saw these ugly worms comin' out of the mountain. Dwarves aren't exactly boatmen, so it took us awhile to come around the river—but we got here as quick as we could!"

Syssal, healed by Sir Ira's spell, stood and stretched, feeling around his chest as if he couldn't believe that the sword wound was gone. "Thanks, old bird," he said to the owl. "I thought for a moment that I was getting my last look at the sky."

"Oh, posh!" Sir Ira demurred. "Though I admit you were losing blood a little too quickly for comfort."

"Blood and lives aplenty were shed today," King Dathwell said sadly, looking around the battlefield. "I had thought, perhaps, that I was done with war. Yet there are times when threats arise from the most unexpected quarter—and we have no choice but to take up arms. For that, I am grateful to have courageous allies, and friends.

"But for now, let us make haste back to the castle. There we will mourn those we have lost, and celebrate the victory that their sacrifice has won."

24
Victory—
Celebration
and Sorrow

"We found the witch of Entropy in the market-place—near where the Daryman suggested," Gazzrick explained as King Dathwell and his companions dismounted in the courtyard of Castle Vanderthan.

"Quite easily," Tellist added, beaming. "After I ceased that accursed levitation, I came down right outside the city. Naturally, it was a matter of simple magic detection to find her ensorceled stall."

"Splendid—splendid!" the monarch chortled, continuing in the good humor he'd felt during the two days' march back to the city.

"Er, not entirely splendid," Gazzrick admitted. "She sort of turned into a big cloud of smoke. . . . I guess she floated away."

"She escaped?" asked Holt.

"Well, how would *you* catch a smoke cloud?" the halfling asked defensively.

"No matter—no matter at all!" declared the king with a dismissive wave. "She's gone, that's the important thing! And with the drubbing we gave her friends, it's not likely she'll be back."

With a shiver, the Daryman remembered the old hag, silently hoping that King Dathwell was right. Yet it was impossible to remain very concerned—after the ride through the cheering crowds of the city, and the knowledge of the great feast that awaited them, such intangible worries seemed like a waste of time.

"And Holton! It's good to see you alive and unhurt!" the halfling declared.

"It's good to be back!" he cried, kneeling to embrace Gazzrick.

"No nicks and cuts? Got all your fingers and toes?" the halfling asked in concern.

"I'm all right," the younger Daryman said, finally straightening. "Though many brave men are not," he added sadly.

"Aye—and it was your son who turned the tide

of the fight," said Fenrald Falwhak, stepping forward as Derek Jaken wheeled up to the group.

"Indeed, Derek—your son is a credit to the traditions of the Darymen," King Dathwell said somberly. "A fact that has not escaped my notice—but more about that tonight." He clapped his hands for attention as Syssal Kipican, Princes Gallarath and Wallas, and Princess Danis all pressed through the crowd that had gathered around.

"Tonight there shall be feasting—feasting for *all!*" declared the king. "Set the tables in the courtyard, and may the spheres spare us rain!"

A cheer rose from the gathered crowd. Danis gave Holt one more victory hug before she headed into the castle to prepare for the feast. Meanwhile the king whispered something to Gazzrick, and then the halfling stepped over to Holt. "I'll find some clothes for you to wear—the king would like you seated at the head table tonight. Oh, and you're both welcome to stay in the same apartment."

"Good . . . kinda got used to those girls combin' my hair for me," said the elder Daryman with a wink.

Mystified and intrigued by the king's invitation, Holt and Fenrald made their way with Derek to the chambers in the castle. They spent the time before the feast telling Gazzrick about their nearly disastrous quest for the Black Goat. "We brought back one sackful of the wine," Holt concluded. "I hope he can be satisfied with that."

"Somehow I think it will do," the halfling agreed.

Trumpets brayed the invitation to feast, and when the two farmers and the dwarf arrived in the courtyard they were astounded by the transformation. Tables and benches filled the great expanse, which teemed with people from the city as well as those who lived in the castle. Torches and lanterns flared on the walls, casting gentle illumination across the throng.

Together with the royal family, Holt was joined by Fenrald, Syssal Kipican, Prince Gallarath, and his brother, Wallas, at the head table. Everyone was in fine spirits—especially the king, who personally filled Holt and Fenrald's glasses from the wineskin.

"Look at this!" crowed Dathwell, sloshing the crimson liquid into all the glasses on the table. "It never gets empty!"

Indeed, Holt saw that the wineskin never seemed to sag—it bulged with the precious drink of the Black Goat even after the king had filled enough glasses to empty it two times over.

"We shall still have the rarest of all wines at your wedding," he teased his daughter. "Apparently it wasn't necessary to bring the goat all the way back here."

"Which would have been quite impossible anyway," Holt muttered to his father, vividly remembering the encircling ring of yetis.

"Though I must claim the honor of capturing the

273

beast—and hence, winning the contest!" Gallarath noted loudly.

The king nodded. "Yes, yes—I've heard about that. You are indeed the winner. But first, there is another matter that demands our royal attention."

An attendant brought Dathwell a bejeweled, ornamental sword. "Rise, Daryman!" he commanded, turning to Holt.

Wonderingly, the young man rose to his feet. Around him he vaguely sensed the crowd falling silent. Mostly he was aware of Danis's eyes, shining with pride, fastened on to his face.

"The matter of noble birth is a thing only the spheres can control—no king can alter that circumstance. However, there are honors that monarchs are given to bestow. The highest of these is Knight Protector of the Realm. Kneel, Holton Jaken."

Numbly, the Daryman did as he was told. King Dathwell lowered the silver blade, touching it once to each of Holt's shoulders.

"Holton Jaken, Daryman of Oxvale, I commend thee for courageous and faultless service in the name of the crown. From now on, you shall be know as Sir Holton of the Lodestone. Know that, among the common-born folk of the realm, there is none who will rank higher!"

Dazed, barely hearing the cheers of the crowd, Holt stood. The honor warmed him—but not enough to break through the chill of the king's other words: 'noble birth' and 'common-born'. These were facts that would never change—and they were facts that would forever stand in the way of his true happiness.

Vaguely he realized that the king was still speaking, though now he had turned to the other side—the side at which sat Prince Gallarath.

". . . an array of noble deeds too extensive to recount here—including his timely arrival on the battlefield with the companies that gave us the margin of victory," Dathwell declared. "But it must be noted that Gallarath of Rochester did in fact capture the Black Goat of the Trollheights, only releasing it upon my daughter's request."

The king's eyes twinkled mischievously as Danis stared intently at her plate. "And I should suggest that the good prince had best get used to my daughter's requests—for it is my pleasure to announce the bonding of Vanderthan and Rochester through the upcoming wedding of the First Daughter and the Crown Prince!"

Dathwell concluded with a flourish, and several courtiers clapped loudly at a few tables in the front. Through his misery, Holt was numbly aware that most of the people of Vanderthan remained conspicuously quiet in light of the momentous announcement.

"Perhaps I wasn't clear." King Dathwell spoke sternly. "I have just—"

"*I* know what you said," Danis replied, finally

raising her eyes to meet her father's. She shifted her gaze to Prince Gallarath. "We are grateful for all that you have done to aid our cause. Your courage, your nobility cannot be faulted—indeed, are worthy of high praise. You've proven yourself a good man, honest and loyal—and I am honored to call you my friend."

The princess stood, her voice growing stronger. "But please know this, my father, and my good prince. I cannot, I *will* not, marry you."

Through the stunned silence of the courtyard the only sound was that made by Fenrald Falwhak glugging a few quick sips of wine. Abruptly the king cleared his throat, his face growing stern.

"Now, my dear, I have tried to be a tolerant father to you. But there are some things incumbent upon royalty—you must think of more than—"

"It's no use speaking about it, Father. My mind is made up!"

"It's *his* fault!" cried Gallarath, standing so quickly that his chair toppled backward. The prince extended an accusing finger at Holt. "It's the farmboy who has twisted her senses!"

The Daryman stood as abruptly, sticking out his chin as he turned to the red-faced prince. A part of Holt was elated by Danis's stance, while another part flushed with nearly uncontrollable anger. "I've twisted nothing! The princess can make up her mind by herself—when she's looking at an over-inflated peacock, she knows what she sees!"

Now it was Prince Wallas who rose, standing beside his brother and shaking his fist at Holt. "Such insults against the house of Rochester shall not be borne. If my brother declines to fight you, than you'll taste my steel."

"I do not decline—indeed, I demand satisfaction from the Daryman!" cried Gallarath.

"I'll fight you both!" Holt snarled, carried away by his own anger. "In whatever order, or at the same time!"

"Stop! Stop it!" Danis shouted. "You're acting like fools! Or peacocks!" She astonished Holt by glaring furiously at him. "You're *all* peacocks, strutting and posing and dueling as if you think that has anything to do with . . . with *anything!*"

Sobbing, she whirled away from the table and ran into the garden. King Dathwell, glowering, looked after his daughter and then turned his displeasure toward Gallarath and Holt. For long, slow heartbeats, nobody made a sound. The Daryman's anger slipped further away with each moment, until he felt very foolish.

"Your Majesty . . . I apologize," he said slowly. "My temper has led me to act, well, just as your daughter said." He bowed stiffly to Prince Gallarath. "I meant no offense to you, or to your house or your name. All of us understand the contributions Rochester made to this victory—and I, too, would number you among my friends, if you will let me."

The noblemen scowled for a moment, but then he returned Holt's bow with a nod of his head. "Perhaps I, too, was hasty. Let it be known to all that in the thick of the battle this Daryman saved my life, at great risk to his own. And, if there's a thing I learned over the journey to the Troll-heights, it is that the First Daughter of Vander-than will tolerate no man giving her orders. Not me, not her father, and not a Daryman."

Holton looked toward the garden, acutely conscious of Danis's misery—and his own part in causing it. "Sire," he said. "I beg your permission to seek the princess and offer my apology to her, as well."

Dathwell hesitated, with a sidelong glance at Gallarath. The prince looked away, clearly uninterested in pursuing the distraught woman through the maze of the garden. "Er, very well. Someone should talk to her."

The Daryman tried hard not to run as he left the banquet, though once he reached the maze of hedges he broke into a trot. As he had known he would, he found Danis beside the pool in the garden's center. She sat quietly on a bench, staring at the water, barely looking up as he advanced to stand before her.

"I—I came to apologize," he said. "I should not have lost my temper. Your father was acting only as a good king. It is not for me to interfere—"

"You're right—I need no one to make my argu-

ments for me," she said. "But then you had to threaten to fight that—that *peacock!*"

"It was his ill-mannered assumption," Holt declared. "As if he *deserved* your hand!"

"But you didn't have to *fight* him!" she replied fiercely. "Why, you could have been terribly hurt—*killed* even! And then—"

"You thought I would have *lost?*" the Daryman demanded indignantly. "Why, it would have been the prince who suffered the taste of my sword! And his peacock brother, too!"

"You men!" the princess cried in exasperation. "Who'll stab who? Who cares? Why does it always have to be a fight!" She stood up and glared at him, her eyes a few inches from his face.

Even a few seconds later he couldn't remember how it happened: one moment they were glaring belligerently, and then the next his arms were around her shoulders. She drew close to him. Her face turned up to his, and in the moonlight he was positively stunned by her beauty—as if he had never seen her before.

Their lips met, tentatively at first and then with greater force, and for Holton Jaken everything else in the world ceased to exist.

Epilogue

"I win!" cackled Pusanth, giving Dalliphree a good-natured slap on the back—a slap that nearly knocked the fairy into the pool.

"Oh, flummox!" she retorted, buzzing upward even as the image of Castle Vanderthan, of all Karawenn, faded from the clear water. "It wasn't fair!"

"No backing out of this one," the sage noted, still chortling. "The bet was fairly made, and fairly won!"

"Well, all right," sulked Dalliphree. "But that just means that we've *each* won one game with these mortals! So, there—we're tied!"

281

Suitors Duel

"Aye, we are." Pusanth's eyes narrowed as he looked at the water. "But for how long?"